GHOST DANCE

When Sarah Clinton asks John Galley to avenge the death of her father, the bounty killer accepts the job immediately. Taking on a vicious outlaw like Red McCready is exactly the kind of job he's been looking for. But the hunt is complicated as Galley meets some Sioux Indians, who enlist his help in protecting the secret of their sacred mountain. Before he trades lead with the outlaw, they insist that he takes part in the mystical Ghost Dance, when he comes face to face with his deadly past.

D1809939

Books by Adam Wright
in the Linford Western Library:

BLACK RIVER

ADAM WRIGHT

GHOST DANCE

Complete and Unabridged

LINFORD
Leicester

First published in Great Britain in 1997 by
Robert Hale Limited
London

First Linford Edition
published 2001
by arrangement with
Robert Hale Limited
London

British Library CIP Data

Wright, A. (Adam)
    Ghost dance.—Large print ed.—
Linford western library
    1. Western stories
    2. Large type books
    I. Title
    823.9'14 [F]

    ISBN 0–7089–4592–9

Published by
F. A. Thorpe (Publishing)
Anstey, Leicestershire

Set by Words & Graphics Ltd.
Anstey, Leicestershire
Printed and bound in Great Britain by
T. J. International Ltd., Padstow, Cornwall

This book is printed on acid-free paper

For Edward Wood and
John Godward, the pioneers.

And for B.J.

1

Creeping stealthily along the rocky ridge, John Galley wondered if tonight might be his last night alive. He paused and strained his ears to hear the sound he had picked up moments ago; the sound of his enemy. The moonlit night was quiet.

He had been tracking Bill Holmes for five days now and he worried that the outlaw might know he was being hunted. Sometimes a man can sense these things. The folks back in Julesburg, where Holmes had robbed the stagecoach, said the man was as cunning as a wounded coyote. Galley wondered if coming face to face with such a hardcase was worth four hundred dollars. It wasn't much money.

Galley knew that a man like Holmes could kill him easily.

He realised that he didn't care.

He topped the ridge and dropped to his hands and knees, crawling through a carpet of pine needles. Their scent was sharp and strong. Another smell reached him, drifting on the gentle night breeze: cooking meat.

Galley crept to an outcropping of rock and peered around. Below, in the trees, he caught the orange flicker of a fire. He had caught up with his man at last. Keeping low among the pines, he turned and headed back down the ridge.

He eased his Colt from its holster, the leather creaking slightly. Out here, in the still night, the sound seemed too loud and Galley grimaced. He stalked forward to the fire in the trees. When he was twenty yards from the flickering flames, he pressed himself to the trunk of a tree. A man sat by the fire.

A rabbit carcass hung over the flames on a spit, its fat dripping into the fire and hissing angrily. The smell of the meat was stronger now that he was nearer the fire and Galley realised he hadn't eaten since this morning. He had been too busy tracking his quarry to eat. The man was dressed in buckskin and sat facing the fire, his back to Galley. He seemed unaware of the bounty hunter's presence.

Galley raised the Colt. Its metal edge shone with a ghostly phosphorescence in the moonlight.

He shouted, his voice cutting through the stillness of the night. 'That you, Bill Holmes?'

The man by the fire did not move, did not jump up, startled, in fact did not move an inch.

Galley edged closer, away from the tree he had been using for cover. 'Holmes?' he asked again.

He felt his stomach knot. His nerves screamed at him to run. He felt too exposed in the bright ghostly moonlight. His grip on the Colt tightened, became too tight. He almost squeezed off a shot but regained his composure enough to stop himself doing that at least. A sound in the trees behind him startled him and he whirled around, realising too late what the unmistakable sound had been: a rifle being cocked.

Bill Holmes stood before him, dressed in a dirty grey shirt. He pointed a Remington rifle at Galley's stomach. 'You looking for me?' he asked. His voice was gravelly, calm. 'You think Billy Holmes is some animal to be hunted down? I knew you was following me a day back. You ain't much good at your job, boy. What you been creeping up on ain't more'n my jacket and hat propped up by the fire. Lower that gun.'

Galley let the hand holding the Colt fall to his hip. 'Stage company at Julesburg says you're worth four hundred dollars, Holmes.'

Holmes grinned and it was not a pretty sight. Most of his teeth were rotten and brown from chewing tobacco. The grin did not reach his eyes. They remained cold and hard.

'That's a strange accent for these parts, boy. That English?'

Galley remained silent. He had hoped his English accent was fading. Perhaps when it was gone entirely, he would be able to forget finally. He didn't really believe it of course. He would never forget. Until he was dead. Which may be in the next few moments.

A dark look of anger flashed across the outlaw's face and he lifted the rifle slightly, aiming at Galley's face. 'You think I'm not worth talkin' to, boy? You think huntin' men is more honest than robbin' stages?' His finger tightened on the Remington's trigger.

Galley brought the Colt up without thinking, his body moved automatically, as if he were a dancer who had executed this movement a hundred times before and had perfected it. The revolver arced upwards, glinting in the moonlight, as he dropped to one knee, below the aim of the rifle. The movement was swift and fluid. If the Remington had been pointed at his stomach, Galley would have been shot before he could get below the rifle's range of fire. But he didn't think about that. He didn't think about anything, simply allowed his body to act automatically, perfectly.

A look of surprise creased Holmes' features and he lowered the Remington as the Colt spat noisily, destroying the quiet stillness of the night.

Holmes spun backwards, a red stain appearing on his shirt like a blossoming red rose. He fired the Remington at a pine tree, as if in the excitement he had forgotten about Galley altogether and bark exploded with a loud crack.

Galley squeezed the Colt's trigger again and Holmes sprawled headlong to the ground. He lay still among the pine needles and splinters of bark. The rifle clattered to the ground several feet away, near the fire where the rabbit spat angrily.

Standing over Holmes, Galley holstered the Colt. 'You should have been quicker,' he said to the body. His pulse throbbed within his temples and his muscles twitched excitedly. Any other man would feel grateful to still be alive at this moment. But not Galley.

He walked over to the fire and retrieved the buckskin coat and hat. They were propped up with pine branches. Holmes had almost trapped him with the ruse. He lay the coat over the prone body and placed the hat over the face, which still looked surprised, even in death.

He walked back to the rocky ridge where he had left his horse and led it to the campsite. After a few minutes searching in the forest, he found Holmes' pinto and tethered it next to his own.

Unrolling a blanket from his saddle-bag, he sat by the fire and removed the rabbit from the spit. As he tore into the hot, succulent meat he glanced at the buckskin-covered body and wondered at the line of work he found himself in. He had killed Holmes for four hundred dollars; he had killed men for a lot less. Maybe they deserved this quick justice, and if he was able to deliver it, why did he feel so angry with himself every time he killed someone for money?

He knew the answer, of course, but refused to dwell on it now. He would not think of Emma. Her memory only came when he had drunk too much rye and his mind wandered to places it dare not go when he was sober.

He finished the rabbit and tossed the remains into the dying fire. He had a long ride ahead of him in the morning and he had best get some sleep. He lay down on the blanket, staring up at the bright silver moon and stars in the clear Colorado sky.

Soon, he was asleep and dreaming of things he dared not think of when awake.

2

The commotion outside her room at the Two Gun Saloon woke Sarah Clinton. She dressed hurriedly and, squinting against the strong morning sunlight, pulled back the red drapes and stared at the main drag below. The law office was situated directly opposite the Two Gun and, outside, a crowd was gathering, gravitating toward a man who was leading two horses down the main drag. The horse in the lead was riderless; the second had a body draped in buckskin strapped to its saddle.

Sarah rushed from the room and down the creaky wooden stairs which led to the ground floor. She had been in Julesburg three days looking for a specific type of man who might take the job she had to offer. Many of the local men had bragged about their abilities with guns and tracking, but when she had told them the nature of the job, they had blanched and taken back their words, not willing to discuss the matter any further. Perhaps this man, obviously a bounty hunter by trade, would help her. The fact that he was bringing a dead man to the marshal's office was proof of his ability.

She had taken a room at the Two Gun precisely because it was opposite the law office and offered her more chance of finding the type of man she needed. She had even endured the way the saloon owner, an elderly man with a wife, leered at her every time he saw her. Finally, her search might be at an end.

Sarah reached the ground floor and the owner looked at her from behind the bar. 'Howdy, ma'am.' He grinned lecherously at her as she walked past him. She could feel his eyes watching her as she stepped out into the sunlight.

The man was unstrapping the body from the horse now, and a crowd of townspeople watched him curiously.

'Yep, that's Bill Holmes all right,' she heard an old man say.

The bounty hunter, a tall, lean man with dark hair and grey eyes ignored the crowd and carried the body into the marshal's office. He had a slight limp and favoured his right leg. Sarah turned to the nearest woman and asked, 'Who is that man?'

The woman shrugged. 'He was passing through town when news came that Bill Holmes, the dead man, had robbed a stage headed for Antelope. He just upped and took off after him. His friend stayed behind after he left, though.'

'Friend?'

The woman pointed at an elderly man who was leading the bounty hunter's horses down the main drag, toward the livery stable at the far end of town.

Sarah walked after the man, leaving the babbling crowd behind, and soon caught up with him. 'Excuse me, do you know the man who brought that body to the marshal?'

The old man was short and bespectacled with a wisp of white hair that curled over his forehead. He nodded. 'That's John Galley. He's a bounty hunter.'

'Are you his partner?'

The old man laughed. 'Well, I wouldn't say that exactly. Can't handle a gun myself.' He held up one hand. 'Joints won't let me hold anything much more. Except maybe shot glasses.' A shadow of sadness passed over his face and he seemed to be remembering older, better times.

'But you do know about him? You know what he's capable of?'

He nodded again. 'John Galley's capable of a lot of things, Miss. I've known him for a fair few years. I look after his affairs and horses. He needs more than one 'cos he never knows when he has to go off. He has to alternate them.' He narrowed his eyes. 'You ain't looking for no romance, are ya?'

She felt herself blush and shook her head. Galley sounded like the man she needed to help her. 'I've got a job that he might like to take on.'

The old man thought for a moment then said, 'Well if you tell me what it is and where you're staying, I'll put it to him.'

She shook her head again. 'I want to ask him myself. I'll be at the Two Gun. I've got a room there. If he's interested, tell him to drop by. My name is Sarah Clinton.'

He stuck out his hand. 'Wiley Jones.'

'Wiley?'

He laughed. 'Real name's Will Jones. John started calling me Wiley some time back and it stuck. I'll tell him about your job offer, Miss Clinton.'

'Thank you.' She started back to the Two Gun, then looked at the clear sky and decided to take a walk around town instead. She knew that men like John Galley and Wiley Jones lived from hand to mouth and needed all the money they could get. She was sure they would accept her offer. She headed in the direction of the town stores. The day was looking brighter all the time.

★ ★ ★

The marshal looked up from his desk and said, 'Don't bring that in here.'

Galley shrugged. The body was heavy in his arms. 'You want me to leave it out in the sun. It'd stink up your town some.'

The marshal, a heavy man with a thick drooping moustache sighed and leaned back in his chair. He looked as if the last thing he had wanted to see this morning was a bounty hunter carrying a body through his door. 'OK, put it down over there.' He indicated the corner of the room.

Galley put the body down on the floor and walked back to the marshal's desk. 'Bill Holmes,' he said thumbing over his shoulder. 'Robbed the Denver stage five days ago and now worth four hundred dollars.'

'And just who the hell are you?' the marshal asked.

'John Galley,' Galley held out his hand but the marshal ignored it. Galley had seen this type of man before. Some lawmen recognised that bounty hunters were necessary, delivering justice after the law had run out of resources. Others, like the man in front of him, Galley guessed, hated bounty hunters because they saw them as an admission that the law was fallible and needed outside help. He didn't care to theorise on the fallibility or otherwise of the law; he just wanted his money, a bath and sleep in a real bed. Wiley would be taking care of his horses now, so he had nothing to attend to before getting some rest after a long time out riding.

Except getting his money.

The marshal looked at the body, then back at Galley and shook his head slowly. 'The stage company that put up the reward is based in Denver. I'm going to have to wire them to see about your money. Meantime, you'll have to stick around. Now I'm not happy about that. We don't have much trouble here and I want to keep it that way.'

'I don't cause trouble,' Galley said evenly.

'Trouble is your business, son.'

Galley shook his head. 'My business is cleaning up the mess after the trouble's over.'

He stalked out of the law office, leaving the marshal to deal with the body of Bill Holmes.

★ ★ ★

He was sitting at a table in the Two Gun and drinking a bottle of rye when Wiley found him. He had walked out of the marshal's office and spotted the saloon directly across the main drag. That had been half an hour and half a bottle ago. Wiley sat opposite him. He looked worried.

'You tended to the horses?' he asked Wiley.

Wiley nodded. 'Did Holmes put up

much of a fight?'

Galley shook his head. He realised that the only reason he was sitting here now was because of his body's instinctual survival reflex. Sometimes it acted against his own interests. Holmes was dead now, his life now no more than a dream, but his own life went on, a stark nightmare. He tried to throw the memory out of his mind but the rye was giving it a place to stay.

Wiley looked around nervously. 'You get the dinero?'

'Marshal has to wire to Denver before he releases it.' He looked closely at Wiley. In all the years he had known the old man, he had never seen him look so nervous. 'What's the matter?'

Wiley looked down at the scarred table. 'Nothing.'

'Come on, Wiley, you can be straight with me. What is it?'

Wiley cleared his throat and hesitated, as if picking his words carefully. Then, he said, 'I seen a lady this morning, just after you rode in and she was asking about you. Says she has a job.'

Galley took a drink. 'What's wrong with that? We could use the cash.'

Wiley looked even more nervous now, as if he thought Galley wouldn't like what he was going to say next. He adjusted his small, round glasses and traced his finger along one of the deep scratches in the table and didn't look up as he spoke. 'After I got the horses cleaned up, I asked around to see if anyone knew about this job. Maybe she'd spoke to others before me. Seems she had, all right. But no one was fool enough to take the job because it's a sure trail to Hell.'

Galley sat up slightly. This sounded like what he had been looking for all these years; something which would finally kill the memory which haunted him day and night.

Maybe a trail to Hell is what I deserve.

Maybe.

Wiley went on. 'Seems she had some

18

sort of altercation with Red McCready. She's looking for some fool to go after him.'

Galley shrugged. 'What's wrong with that?'

'You know that Red McCready is a vicious dog. No telling how many people he's killed just for the hell of it. And he's riding with Tom Riley and Bill Jakes, two more hardcases. No matter what this lady's offering for Red, it ain't worth it.'

Galley took a hit of rye. It burned his throat and warmed his stomach. 'Tell her I'll take the job.'

Wiley looked up at him angrily. 'I knew you'd say that! John, listen to me. You remember what state you was in when I met you in Mexico? You was burned out, wasted. I could have left you dying in that alley. But I helped get you back on your feet and for a while, you seemed to have recovered from whatever it was that was troubling you. But now, it's come back. I can see it in your eyes, the way you sometimes stare

19

off as if you're somewhere else. And, when we're on the trail, I've heard you talking in your sleep.'

Galley was shocked. No one knew what was in his mind; it was a secret, locked away. He had no idea that Wiley might know something. 'What do I say when I'm asleep?'

Wiley looked concerned. 'Not much, but I don't like what I have heard and it worries me. You're just waiting for one of these jobs to kill you and now you've got the chance. There's no way you can take Red McCready. Anyone with the sense of a dog would refuse the job. But I knew you'd take it. You're gonna let Red McCready kill you like the damn fool you are.'

The old man slumped back in his seat, as if the angry outburst had taken its toll on him. Galley looked at him and realised that Wiley really did worry after him. Perhaps if the old man knew the truth, he might not be so bothered about what happened to John Galley after all.

'Think about it, John,' he said.

'I have. She must be offering good dinero for this job and we could use it.'

Wiley shook his head slowly. He seemed to know it would be useless to try to change Galley's mind. 'Ain't no good if you ain't alive to spend it.' He stood up and stretched, the bones in his back popping loudly. 'The lady's got a room here; I'll see if she's here and we can get more lowdown on this damn fool job.'

He left the table and Galley took another hit of booze. He had heard of Red McCready; most bounty hunters had. Red was an outlaw who had been active for four or five years. It was said that he killed for fun as much as for anything else. He was called Red on account of his shock of red hair. Either that or the fact that he left a trail of blood wherever he went.

Wiley returned. 'She ain't here. I got you a room so's you can rest. You look like you need it.' He threw a room key onto the table. 'I'll have a couple of drinks and wait for the lady to come back.'

Galley rose from the table and, clutching the room key in one hand and the rye bottle in the other, climbed the creaky stairs to the rooms on the first floor. He was tired and sleep in a bed would be welcome. But he feared what dreams would come with that sleep.

★ ★ ★

Sarah Clinton felt elated at the prospect of John Galley going after Red McCready. As she returned to the Two Gun Saloon, she took a detour which took her to the edge of town. She watched the horizon, where the sun was spreading golden light over the pine forests, and she thought, You're out there somewhere, Red McCready. I'm coming to get you and I'm bringing a bounty hunter with me. You can't get away with what you did to my family.

She walked back toward town and made her way to the Two Gun. She would wait in her room for Wiley and Galley, away from the staring eyes of the saloon owner. But as she stepped through the saloon's batwings, she noticed Wiley sitting at a corner table, nursing a drink. She walked over and sat opposite him. 'Hello, Mr Jones.'

He smiled. 'You can call me Wiley, Miss.'

'Have you spoken with John Galley yet?'

He nodded. 'Listen, Miss, I'm gonna be straight with ya. I don't think John should take on the kind of job you have in mind.'

She frowned. 'But I haven't told you what the job is yet.'

'No, Miss, but I've been asking about and it seems you're looking for someone to kill Red McCready.'

Sarah hadn't realised the old man might ask around about the nature of the job. Still, he would have known sooner or later. She waited for Wiley to tell her that the job was too dangerous and any man would be a fool to go after

Red McCready. That was what all of the town's drunken braggards had told her; any man who went after Red was either suicidal or over confident of his abilities to handle a gun. In this untamed land, both amounted to the same thing.

'So now you're going to tell me you won't take the job, just like everyone else,' she said.

He shook his head slowly. 'No, Ma'am. I've spoken to John and he said he'd go after Red.'

'But I haven't told you how much I'm offering.'

'Doesn't matter to John,' Wiley said. He looked tired. 'He's not doing this for the cash, although he could use it right now. He's doing this for reasons of his own.'

'What reasons?'

The old man shrugged. 'I wish I knew. I met John a few years ago in Mexico. He was hurting bad, just another drunk trying to lose himself in a bottle. But there was something different about John; there was something about him that told a fella he was hurting more than the others.'

Wiley took a sip of his drink. 'So I helped him some. I had a job as a ranch hand and I got John a job there too. Turned out I was right about there being something about John that set him apart from the rest; he was damn good with guns. Quick and accurate and calm. He's a born shootist. Anyhow, John seemed OK for a while, then one day something happened that brought back his troubles.'

Sarah leaned forward over the table. She hadn't realised John Galley could be a troubled man. He had looked so confident this morning when he had brought Bill Holmes's body to the law office.

Wiley went on. 'We were out working the ranch one day, rounding up the cattle, with Zach Jones the ranch owner when one of his sons comes riding up saying come back to the ranch house quick. We go tearing off to the house, me, John and Zach, and when we get there, we find Zach's wife, Wilma, sprawled out on the kitchen floor. She'd been cooking supper and she'd had a stroke. There was carrots and sweet potatoes all over the floor where she'd fallen.'

He paused and took another sip of his drink, shaking his head and frowning as if perplexed. 'Of course, Zach was cut up over losing his missus and we was all upset; Wilma Jones had been a real nice old woman. But John's reaction to her passing was strange. He kept staring at her lying there on the floor and it was like something in his mind just flipped over. He kept staring at Wilma's body and that troubled look that I had seen in his eyes in Mexico came back. That night, he told me he was heading out to become a bounty hunter. I decided to go with him, to look out for him as much as anything else. He had changed again, returned to his old ways of thinking. He's dangerous when he's like this. A danger to

26

himself as well as others.'

Sarah wondered if it was wise to hire John Galley. If he really was unstable, it might not be a good idea. Still, she had no choice; no one else would take the job; Red's reputation as a merciless killer made sure of that. John Galley was her final hope. She wondered what kind of experience could make a man like John Galley, who appeared to all outward appearances to be calm and confident, unstable and self-destructive in his thinking. She asked Wiley.

The old man shrugged. 'I don't rightly know. Sometimes I've heard him talking to himself in his sleep but I only catch bits and scraps and it doesn't make much sense to me.'

'What have you heard?'

He shrugged again. 'Nothing much. All I know is that something happened in Canada a while back and it involved a woman. John's never even told me he's been to Canada, but that's what he talks about when he's having his nightmares.'

'He seems so calm,' Sarah said.

'He hides his troubles well. In his line of business, it doesn't pay to have folks thinking you got a weakness. Why do you want Red McCready dead anyhow?'

She tried to hold back her own bad memories. 'He killed my father a month ago. He . . . ' She stopped as she spotted Galley coming down the stairs. He still looked tired and she wondered what nightmares he had dreamed during his sleep. He came over to the table and sat down. Wiley made the introductions and Sarah looked closely at Galley for the first time.

His face was lined from riding long hours out in the elements but he was still handsome. His grey eyes seemed like a calm ocean, but she knew that there were tumultuous undercurrents beneath their placid appearance. His face seemed kindly, not the face of a bounty hunter and killer of men at all and she wondered again what had changed this man and turned him into what he was.

'Miss Clinton was saying that Red McCready killed her father,' Wiley said.

Galley nodded and sat back in his chair, waiting for her to continue.

'My father owned a small ranch north of Blue Water Creek and we worked it together. My mother died of pneumonia when I was very young and I don't remember her at all; my father brought me up on his own. We worked the ranch, which was situated in the shadow of a small mountain range. We were happy there until one day Red McCready came riding out to our ranch, spinning a crazy yarn about there being a cache of money being hidden in a cave in the mountains. He said an outlaw by the name of Ed Laymon held up the bank at Denver and hid the money in the mountains.

'I've heard that story,' Galley interrupted. 'He left the money there and was shot by a posse of lawmen before he could return to fetch it.'

Sarah nodded. 'The mountain is

called Laymon's Peak. A lot of men searched for the cache but none had any luck. But Red McCready told my father he knew the location of it, offered to split the takings fifty-fifty with him if he helped him collect the stash.'

'Why not just keep his mouth shut and take all the money for himself?' Wiley asked.

'I think he wanted my father out of the way. They went off to the mountains leaving me to keep the ranch running. My father had his Winchester rifle.'

'And Red killed him?' Galley asked.

'He must have. After they left, I became worried. My father had taken the Winchester but we also had a Remington Repeater and I loaded it and waited. I *knew* something was going to happen and that I'd need the rifle. I sat on the porch with the rifle on my lap and eventually Red came back from the mountains. It was getting dark. He had his gun out and started shooting at me. I barely made it back into the house. I fled to the stables and rode out of there.'

'You're lucky to be alive,' Wiley observed.

She nodded. 'I didn't dare go back to the ranch, so I've been looking for someone to help me get Red. That ranch is all my father ever dreamed of. I can't abandon it to that dirty outlaw.'

Galley nodded. 'He wanted you and your father off the land for some reason. He probably has a hideout somewhere near Laymon's Peak. It's a good area. The land to the north of the mountains is Indian, so not many folk would go out there. It's a good place to start. I'll head out in the morning.'

'I'm going with you,' Sarah said.

Galley shook his head. 'You'll wait here until I get back or you hear news that I'm never coming back.'

Sarah had expected his refusal to take her with him, but she was determined to press her point. 'Mr Galley, Red

31

McCready killed my father and tried to kill me as well. I want to be there when you kill him.'

Galley looked steadily at her. 'And if I can't?'

'Then I'll take my chances. At least I'll die knowing that I tried to avenge my father.'

Galley sighed. 'All right but I go into the mountains alone. There could be Indians up there and if they catch a hold of you, you'll wish Red McCready's aim had been better when he shot at you.'

She nodded. 'I'll wait at the ranch house.'

'And I want Wiley along to look after you,' Galley said.

'I'm not helpless,' she protested, 'I can look after myself.'

'All the same,' Galley said, 'Wiley's coming along. He can just about shoot straight and we may need all the firepower we can get.' He stood up. 'I'm going over to pay the marshal a visit and see if my four hundred dollars has been cleared yet.' He strode out of the saloon.

Sarah watched him go. She would be glad to get out of Julesburg and away from the saloon owner's lecherous gaze but what kind of trouble was she letting herself in for?

3

As he left the saloon, Galley wondered if he was doing the right thing by letting Sarah Clinton come along on the hunt for Red McCready. Of all the jobs he had undertaken, this was potentially the deadliest. He also regretted the fact that Wiley would be coming. The old man was a good, kind person and Galley knew he did not deserve such a friend. But he needed Wiley to look after Sarah and keep her out of trouble. She seemed to be a very spirited woman. Galley prayed he wasn't leading them both to their deaths.

The marshal was standing on the boardwalk smoking a pipe as Galley approached him. He looked at the bounty hunter and Galley noticed a frown crease his forehead. 'Afternoon, marshal,' he said as amiably as possible.

The marshal nodded.

'Any news on my money yet?'

The marshal shook his head.

'You know, the sooner I get it, the sooner I leave your town.'

The marshal puffed on his pipe and watched the passers-by going about their business. Galley waited. Finally, the marshal sighed and said, 'All right, Mister, I'll get on the telegraph this afternoon. Where can I find you?'

Galley surveyed the buildings along the main drag, then pointed at a gambling house called The Lucky Wheel. 'I'll be in there.' He walked across the drag and into the gambling house. Wiley would be dealing with the horses and settling up the account at the Two Gun, so he had time to unwind with a game of poker.

The Lucky Wheel was dark and dingy, with a bar at the far end of the room and gambling tables scattered here and there. In the centre of the room sat a roulette wheel, currently spinning, the steel ball clattering through the numbers. Four men stood around the wheel and a few were playing cards at the surrounding tables. A man dressed in a white shirt and pin-striped trousers approached Galley. 'You'll have to check your guns at the door, Sir.'

Galley turned around and noticed a counter by the door where a slight man with a wispy moustache sat watching him. Galley removed his Colt from his belt and laid it on the counter. It disappeared, with the wispy-moustached man, into a back room. Galley turned back to the gambling tables.

Most of the Wheel's customers were older men, with a couple of women at the roulette table, but at one table, three young men were playing poker. Their table and the surrounding floor were littered with empty glasses and bottles. Galley spoke to the man in the pin-striped trousers. 'Who are those three?'

The man glanced at the table. 'They are the Colton brothers, Sir,' he replied.

'Local ranch hands.' He lowered his voice. 'I wouldn't try to join their game if I were you. They have a bit of a reputation in town as being, shall we say, unfriendly to strangers.'

Galley nodded, looked around the establishment, then went over to the Colton brothers' table. He slumped into a seat and nodded. 'Howdy.'

The three brothers looked up from their cards. Two wore dark, straggly beards and were unkempt. The third was fair-haired and seemed slightly younger than his brothers. The smell of alcohol on their breaths was almost overpowering. 'Mind if I pitch in?' Galley asked. The three looked at each other and grinned. The brother sitting opposite Galley nodded.

'Sure, you can pitch in,' he said. 'What's yer name, stranger?'

'John Galley.'

'Well, it's mighty nice to meet ya. I'm Luke and this here's Ned. And this here's our younger brother Todd.' He pushed the deck of cards toward Galley.

Ned and Todd threw their cards onto the deck, abandoning the game they had been playing before Galley showed up.

'I think it's right that newcomers should deal,' Luke said, nodding to the deck of cards and grinning.

'What's yer game?' Ned asked, grinning in the same inane way as his brother.

'How about five-card draw, no wild cards?' Galley said. The dealer always had the advantage in five-card draw because he went last, after being able to gauge his opponents' strengths and weaknesses by observing their discards and bets. The no wild-card rule strengthened this advantage.

However, he knew that by giving himself an advantage, he was asking for trouble. Because when you played against yahoos like the Coltons and started to win, bad things could happen.

He riffled the cards and started to deal.

★　★　★

Shortly after Galley left the Two Gun, Wiley went off to attend to business before they pulled out in the morning. Sarah, pleased to have found someone willing to go after Red McCready, decided to pack her belongings. She climbed the creaky stairs of the Two Gun Saloon and entered her room. Sunlight streamed through the window and Sarah sat on the bed, basking in the warmth. She felt good. Finally, Red McCready was going to pay for what he had done to her father. She felt sure that John Galley, despite his problems, would be a match for McCready. She closed her eyes and relished the warm sunlight on her face. Soon, they would be on the trail and she would be exposed to the elements whether she wanted to be or not.

She heard a creaking on the stairs outside her room.

She opened her eyes. There weren't many other guests staying at the Two

Gun. Perhaps it was Wiley, coming to ask about payment for the job. They hadn't discussed money yet. Or perhaps it was Galley outside, returning after collecting his money from the marshal.

A knock at the door. Short and loud.

'Who is it?' she asked, turning to look toward the door.

Another knock, louder, more insistent.

Had she locked the door? Surely, she must have; she always did. But her mind had been on other things when she'd entered the room. Perhaps she had forgotten. The key was still in the door on this side. She could go over to it and twist it just to make sure. But she suddenly did not feel like going near the door. 'Who is it?' she called out again.

Silence.

Sarah felt a wave of panic rise inside her. She realised she was gripping the covers of the bed; they were bunched up beneath her hands.

'Is there anyone there?' she called,

trying hard to calm her voice but failing. She cursed herself for sounding frightened.

Silence.

Perhaps there was no one after all. Her grip on the bedspread relaxed slightly.

The key fell from the keyhole and struck the wooden floor with a metallic *clink*.

She heard another key enter the lock and turn, unlocking the door. She had locked it, but the intruder on the other side had a key to her room.

She searched around the room for a weapon to defend herself with. Her father's Remington was in the wardrobe at the foot of the bed, unloaded. By the time she could load it, the intruder would be in the room.

She glanced around in panic but before she located a makeshift weapon, the door burst open. The proprietor of the saloon stood in the doorway, breathing heavily and watching her. 'I hear you are leaving in the morning,' he said as he closed the door behind him. 'I think before you go, we have a close up talk, eh?' He locked the door and pocketed the key. He was sweating and Sarah could smell whiskey on his breath.

'Look,' she said. 'If you just leave now, I won't tell anyone you were here.' Her voice was trembling now.

He chuckled. 'No one is in the saloon. I locked the doors for a while. I've been watching you since you came here. Pretty. Very pretty.' He moved further into the room, licking his lips. Sarah moved so she was on the opposite side of the bed. 'Now you aren't goin' to be a problem, are you?' he said.

He pulled a straight razor from his pocket and held it up, its blade glinting sharply in the sunlight pouring in through the window. Sarah's eyes widened. She had been hoping to overpower him. He wasn't a large man and he was obviously very drunk, but the razor changed things. Even drunk, he could easily cut her with its blade.

He grinned, licked his lips and, holding the razor in front of him, sprang across the bed at her.

★   ★   ★

Galley held four aces. This was his first good hand. Throughout the game, he had done consistently badly, losing quite a lot of money in the process, and the Coltons had grown in their confidence, increasing their bets with each hand so that a sizeable pile of money now sat on the table.

And Galley's luck had changed. His hand consisted of four aces.

Depending on how you looked at it, his luck had either just got a lot better or a hell of a lot worse. Better, because he had won the pile of money sitting in front of him. Worse, because now the trouble would begin.

'What have ya got?' Luke demanded. He was smiling because a large amount of Galley's money was sitting on the

43

table in front of him and he was sure that he and his brothers had fleeced this unlucky stranger.

Galley looked around the table. All three brothers were waiting for him to show his hand. They were all grinning.

He laid his four aces on the table and they stopped smiling.

Luke looked at him. His face turned an angry purple colour and he snarled. 'You been cheatin'.' The other two Coltons wore angry looks as well.

'No,' Galley said. 'I just had a run of luck.' His hand dropped instinctively to his gunbelt but of course his gun was hanging up in the back room. He hoped the Coltons' pieces were in there as well, next to his own.

A silence descended throughout the Lucky Wheel. Everyone's attention was upon the Coltons and Galley. Even the roulette wheel stopped spinning. 'Well, I guess this money is mine,' Galley said, reaching for the pile of crumpled notes and dirty coins on the table.

'Not so fast.' Luke slapped a meaty

hand on top of Galley's and pinned it to the table. The Colton reached into his shirt and his hand re-emerged holding a derringer. Galley looked into the twin, tiny barrels which stared at him like the black eyes of Death. The gun only had two shots, but one shot was enough to kill a man.

Maybe I'm going to get shot over a few dollars.

Maybe.

'Put the gun away, Luke,' someone at the roulette table said. 'He ain't armed so that ain't fair.'

'Cheatin' ain't fair,' Luke said and Galley saw the anger rise in him and knew that he was going to pull the trigger on the derringer.

Maybe now I die.

No.

He pushed forward with his legs, forcing his way out of his chair and pushing over the card table. It tipped over toward Luke and money scattered everywhere, coins raining heavily onto the wooden floorboards. Luke shouted and went flailing backwards as the table tipped. He fired the derringer. The shot went wild and hit the wall.

The interested onlookers now became more interested in their own safety and dived for cover behind chairs and tables. The barman ducked below the bar. Because his hand was still pinned by Luke's, Galley leapt over the table as it tipped. Luke let go of his hand and Galley rolled onto the floor, ending up on the opposite side of the table from where he had just been sitting.

Luke, on his back, grunted angrily and pushed the table away. It smashed to the floor. Ned and Todd were up on their feet and rushing at Galley. He was on his feet as they reached him and he struck Todd in the jaw. The fair-haired Colton brother stumbled away, hurt. Ned reached Galley and lashed out. Galley felt pain arc through his midriff as Ned's blow connected. He doubled over for a moment then managed to punch Ned in the face.

Ned dropped to the floor.

Luke was on his feet now, standing among a pile of scattered money and aiming the derringer again. Galley leaped forward and grabbed his wrist as the derringer cracked and a bullet embedded itself harmlessly in the ceiling. The two men went down, rolling in the coins and bills, struggling against each other.

Galley managed to stagger to his feet and the Coltons gathered together a few feet away, ready to rush him. Galley realised that his advantage of surprise was lost and he had no chance against the three men. He waited for them to come at him.

'What the hell is going on here?' The familiar voice came from the door and everyone turned as the marshal entered, surprise registering on his face as he took in the scene. He saw Galley and the Coltons squaring off and shook his head. 'Now you boys ought to know better. You've been in the jailhouse before for public disturbance. You want to spend tonight there?'

The Coltons shook their heads as one. 'No, Sir,' Luke said. 'We was just havin' some fun with this here stranger.'

'Well take your fun somewhere else. I don't want to see you again today, or you'll be spending the night in a cell. Understood?'

The Coltons muttered amongst themselves and left the Lucky Wheel, each one shooting Galley with a hateful glance on his way out.

The marshal looked at Galley and shook his head. 'I came over here to give you your money. The stage company have OK'd it. Lucky I came by when I did, otherwise I might have had to use that money to bury you. I knew you were trouble the moment I saw you.'

Galley said, 'I told you before, I never start trouble.' He thought for a moment. 'Well, rarely ever.' He held out his hand. 'Can I have my money now?'

'Yeah.' The marshal pushed a wad of notes into his hand and Galley pocketed them. 'Now you can get the hell out of my town. I don't . . . ' He stopped as a woman's scream came from down the street.

The marshal ran out of the Lucky Wheel and toward the Two Gun Saloon, where the sound had come from.

Galley followed as the screaming continued.

★ ★ ★

Sarah screamed as the saloon owner jumped across the bed at her. She quickly sidestepped and he went crashing into the nightstand beside the bed. As he struggled to get up, Sarah rolled across the bed, putting it between them again. She faced him as he stood up again, slicing the razor through the air in front of him. 'Bitch,' he drawled. He lunged across the bed again and she tried to dodge away from him but this time he was ready and he caught her wrist.

49

She screamed again and struggled against his grip but he was too strong for her. He pulled her to the bed.

'Gonna have us some fun,' he whispered excitedly, standing over her.

She struck out with her foot and caught him in the crotch. His breath exploded out of him and he doubled over, sinking to the floor and holding himself. His eyes were streaming with tears of pain.

She wondered if she dared jump over him to get to the door. He might make a grab for her and pull her down with him. He seemed to be in a lot of pain but he might overpower her. And with the razor in his hand, he might slash at her as she tried to get over him.

But she had to get to the door.

She jumped up from the bed and leapt over the prone saloon owner. He didn't grab her or slash at her. He seemed to be hurting a lot. Sarah retrieved her key from the floor near the door. She had to get out fast. She didn't think he would stay down long.

His kind never did.

She grabbed hold of the key and fumbled it into the lock. Her hands were shaking. The metal key chattered into the lock and she twisted it, letting out a breath of relief as the door opened. She flew down the stairs and toward the saloon's main door.

Before she got there, though, the door smashed inwards, coming off its hinges and crashing to the floor. Two men rushed in and Sarah realised that one of them was John Galley. The other, a heavy man, wore a badge and held his gun out as if expecting trouble. He was out of breath, as if he had run a mile to get here.

Galley rushed over to Sarah and took her protectively in his arms. The marshal shouted, 'You all right, Ma'am?'

She nodded and pointed up the stairs, where the Two Gun's proprietor was making his painful way down the stairs, straight razor held loosely in one hand. The marshal appraised the situation and seemed to get an immediate idea of what had happened. He trained his gun on the saloon owner and told him to drop the razor.

Galley, holding Sarah in his arms, asked, 'You sure you're OK?'

'Yes,' she said.

He nodded. 'Good, because the sooner we get out of this town, the better. We've made too many enemies here!'

4

They lit out of town early the next morning. The sun was barely risen, staining the forests and hills orange-yellow when they left Julesburg.

By the time the town was far behind them, the day grew steadily hotter. Galley rode behind Wiley and Sarah, watching as the two talked. The old man seemed to like the lady, and Galley had to admit that he was sort of fond of her himself. Unlike a lot of women he had met, Sarah Clinton knew how to handle herself. She had proved that by the way she had dealt with the owner of the Two Gun Saloon. She knew how to handle a horse, too. She rode like an expert rider, obviously a skill acquired while working her father's ranch.

Also, she was mighty pretty.

Galley tried to ignore that fact. He hardly ever associated with women; his job meant he had to spend much of his life alone on the trail of killers and thieves. That suited him fine. But of the few women he had known, Sarah was certainly the prettiest. She had tied her hair back before they left Julesburg, and Galley found himself watching the way her pony tail flicked back and forth behind her back. The movement was hypnotic.

I'd better stop thinking that way.

Why?

Remember what happened in Canada.

He pushed the thought from his mind. He didn't *want* to remember what happened in Canada. And, of course, that was why he limited his contact with women; they brought back the memories of Emma Holt. So why had he let Sarah come along? Was he trying to exorcise some demon by facing his fears head on? No, because no matter how much he faced his fears, he couldn't change what had happened in Canada. He rode up to Wiley and Sarah. 'We should be near the railroad soon,' he said. 'We'll rest there before pushing on for Blue Water Creek.'

'Mr Galley, we haven't discussed the matter of payment for the job,' Sarah said.

'You can call me John, Ma'am. Talk the payment terms over with Wiley,' he replied. 'He handles the business side of things.'

'And you handle the killing.'

He nodded. 'Yep.'

'Who would you say has the easier job?' she asked.

Wiley laughed. 'She's sure inquisitive, John.'

'No contest,' Galley answered. 'Wiley has to deal with figures and balancing accounts while all I got to do is shoot straight. I got the easier job by far.'

She frowned. 'You think killing someone is easy?'

He nodded. 'Yep. Easy.'

Then a memory stung him and he added, 'Sometimes too easy.'

He scanned the horizon and noticed the sun glinting off metal in the distance. 'The railroad's just ahead,' he said. 'There's a place where it cuts through the rocks. We can get some rest in the shade there. The sun'll be directly overhead in a little while.' He rode on, leaving them behind, to scout out the pass.

The pine-covered rocks had been sheared by blasting to make way for the Union Pacific railroad which cut through them. The result was a sheer rock wall, at least fifty feet high, on either side of the tracks. At the far end of the gorge was a dark tunnel, where the rock was so high, the railworkers had decided it was easier to blast a hole through it than try to clear a slice for the track to run through.

The rock walls were topped with pines and the area around the track was in deep, cool shadow. Galley rode into the man-made gorge and the air became instantly cooler and fresher. He took a kerchief from his pocket and mopped the sweat from his brow. Dismounting, he tied his horse to a tree some distance from the track; he didn't want a passing train to scare the animal.

The ground around the track had been scattered with rock chippings and Galley sat down with his back against the sheer, blasted rock. He closed his eyes and let the coolness of the place settle on him.

He took his fixings from his waistcoat and began rolling a smoke. Sitting here, in the shade of the rocks and pines, he understood why men such as himself chose a life roaming around this wild country. A man could feel at peace here. Sometimes, the untamed wilderness could settle even the most troubled mind.

He watched a jay alight on the track. The bird cawed loudly at him before taking wing again.

He wondered what was taking Sarah and Wiley so long to get here. They hadn't been far behind him when he had ridden on. Sticking his flaming cigarillo into his mouth, he walked along the rock wall, his hand resting on the butt of his Colt, which he had retrieved from the Lucky Wheel along with his scattered money before leaving Julesburg.

He reached the edge of the rocks and peeped back the way he had come. There was no sign of Sarah or Wiley. Suddenly uneasy, Galley drew the Colt from its holster. He sprinted back to his horse. If there was going to be trouble, the rail gorge was not a good place to be. If anyone took a shot at him from the top of the rocks, it would be like shooting a fish in a barrel.

He untethered his horse and was about to make his way out of the gorge when a shot rang out from the rocks above. The bullet whacked into the tree which his horse had been tied to moments ago.

He couldn't get out of the gorge. It was too far to the end and he would be too exposed if he made a run for it. Instead, he whirled around and ran the other way, pulling his horse toward the dark tunnel. As he ran, he braced himself for the next shot. Perhaps next time, the shooter wouldn't miss.

It was a short run and he made it but at the tunnel entrance, his horse stopped and pawed the rock chippings on the ground nervously. 'Come on,' Galley coaxed, looking around at the rocks to gauge the location of the shooter. He couldn't see anyone up there. He pulled gently on the reins and the horse took a few hesitant steps into the dark tunnel. He pulled it further, until they were shrouded in blackness.

If the gorge had been cool, the tunnel was as cold as a tomb. Galley could see sunlight at the far end and sunlight through the mouth of the tunnel he had just come through, but in the dark, the air was chilled. His horse pulled nervously on the reins and Galley stroked its ears and spoke softly to it. 'We'll be OK, boy. Well, you will, anyhow. It's me they want, not you. Whoever they are.'

He wondered who might have followed him out here. He had a lot of enemies; his profession saw to that. He looked along the length of the tunnel and realised that he was trapped in here. If there were two or more men out there, all they had to do was come at him simultaneously from each end of the tunnel and he wouldn't have a chance.

He led the horse deeper into the tunnel. If they were going to come at him from each end, he wasn't going to be found straight away; he would be hiding in the darkness.

A figure appeared in the sunlight at the far end of the tunnel. With the light behind the figure's back, Galley didn't recognise the man. He pressed himself against the cold tunnel wall and willed his horse to stay still. He wasn't sure how far into the tunnel the man could see. The figure spoke. 'We got him like a rat in a trap, Luke.' It was Todd Colton.

Those bastards from the Lucky Wheel had followed him. He should have known that those three wouldn't let him leave town without trying to exact some kind of punishment on him.

He turned to look at the other end of the tunnel and a figure had appeared there as well. That figure held a rifle and Galley realised the Coltons were looking for more than just another fight. This figure was taller than Todd and Galley recognised it as Luke Colton. Ned must be the shooter waiting in the rocks above the mouth of the tunnel.

Galley realised he had absolutely nowhere to run and there was no way he could shoot his way out. If he fired at one of the brothers, the other would get him in the back. Despite his self-destructive nature, Galley did not want to die here in this cold tunnel; Sarah and Wiley were depending on him. He dared not think what the Coltons might do to them. Although he had only known Sarah a short time, a part of him already cared for her.

He could not let the Coltons trap him here.

But he had to admit it; his luck had run out on him. His four aces at the Lucky Wheel had been his last piece of good luck but even they had been bad in the end because he might not be here now if not for them.

He felt a pull on the reins as his horse reared up, frightened. It kicked the air and whinnied. 'Easy, boy,' Galley commanded, holding the reins tight. 'What's spooked you?' The horse continued to pull against him.

'I can hear you in there,' Todd Colton called. His voice was nearer. Both men had entered the tunnel and were drawing closer all the time. Galley tried to calm his horse but the animal was almost frantic to get out of the tunnel. 'What's the matter, boy?'

He considered letting the horse go. This was his last stand and there was no need to put the animal through any more discomfort. Galley didn't fear death. His only regret was that Sarah and Wiley would be killed because of him. He cursed himself for leaving them and riding to the gorge without them.

As he was about to let go of the reins, he felt the ground tremble. The horse got even wilder and Galley understood why; a train was coming. He tightened his grip on the reins and pulled the horse close.

He considered his situation as the train approached the tunnel.

Maybe his luck hadn't run out on him after all.

Maybe he still had an ace in the hole.

5

What he had in mind was crazy. Perhaps the most dangerous thing he had ever attempted. But if Sarah and Wiley were to have a chance, he had to try. His biggest problem was the horse. It was so skittish that he wondered if it would let him get into the saddle. He knew the animal had spirit; it was always calm where gunfire was concerned. But trains were something it wasn't used to and it obviously considered them a danger.

Galley hesitated, then resolved himself as he heard the Colton brothers approaching. Very close now. Keeping a strong grip on the reins, he swung himself into the saddle.

The horse bucked slightly but did not attempt to throw him. His weight was familiar to it. His only problem now was controlling the animal. Considering its aversion to trains, what he had in mind was something totally against its nature. He held the reins tightly to stop his hands from shaking. What he had in mind also scared him.

The train noise was thunderous now, shaking the rock walls of the tunnel. The metal track shook and clattered. The horse pulled its head from side to side and pawed the ground but Galley reined it in hard. He had no idea how close the Colton brothers were now. It was too dark to see anything and all he could hear was the train and his own thumping heartbeat. He wondered if he should even be attempting what he was about to do. Perhaps he had finally lost his mind.

The light at the end of the tunnel blacked out as the train engine entered the rock passageway. It was moving slowly and ponderously and that was good because if it had been moving quicker, Galley's idea would have been useless. The horse pulled in the direction of the tunnel mouth which still showed sunlight beyond. 'Easy, boy. Just a few more minutes,' Galley coaxed.

The engine rattled past him in the dark and a stench of burning coal filled the tunnel. Galley felt smoke going into his lungs, and his eyes stung with it. The horse was frantic again and he realised it was now or never.

Instead of resisting the horse's pull, he gave the animal a free rein and it bolted alongside the train, racing to get out of the tunnel ahead of the steel monstrosity which belched foul smoke. Galley let it get up speed until he was sure they were matching the locomotive's speed. He pulled back on the reins to slow the animal's panicky flight and watched the train's cars as they rattled along beside him.

Looking over his shoulder, he noticed an empty cattle car. It was like a huge box on wheels, with a large open doorway on either side. Galley waited until the doorway was level with him and then steeled himself. He was going to try to jump the horse into that car. All depended on his horse's trust now.

Jumping toward a moving train was something that was against every instinct in the animal's body. Still, Galley had no choice. He was relying on the fact that in its blind panic, the horse might follow his command automatically.

He pulled hard on the reins.

The horse jumped.

They landed in the cattle car and the horse's hooves slipped on the floorboards. Still panicking, and probably unaware that it had just jumped onto a moving train, the horse kept going toward the far doorway, threatening to fall off the train. Galley leaned back in the saddle and pulled the reins and the horse stopped, rearing up. Galley lurched out of the saddle and hit the floorboards hard, feeling pain lance up his back.

The horse stopped and turned to regard its fallen rider. Now that it was on the train, the animal seemed calmer.

Galley climbed gingerly to his feet, rubbing his back. The train left the tunnel and sunlight flooded into the car. Galley watched the rocky gorge walls rush by as the train picked up speed. Soon, they were out of the gorge and travelling through pine forests, away from the Coltons and Wiley and Sarah.

Galley patted his horse's neck. His only problem now was getting off the train and getting back to the gorge to help Sarah and Wiley.

★ ★ ★

Ned Colton sat among the rocks, his rifle levelled at Sarah and Wiley. 'Your fella's trapped in the tunnel,' he said. 'No way he's gonna see daylight again.' He chuckled and spat onto the ground.

Sarah realised the predicament she and Wiley were in; without Galley around, they were as good as dead. Wiley, though tough-looking, was no match for the three brothers. And although she was ready to put up a damned good fight, she realised that in the end she would be at the Colton's mercy. And from the look in Ned Colton's eyes as he watched her, she knew what that would involve.

She felt a heavy loss when she considered that John Galley was about to die. Although Wiley had told her about Galley's reckless, almost suicidal nature, she was sure she had seen something deep within the man which clashed with that image. She knew he would be taking a painful secret to his grave. She felt regret because she had hoped to learn his secret and help Galley close that door in his mind which led only to despair.

She barely noticed that the rocks on which they sat were vibrating. She looked down into the gorge as a train, belching thick smoke, slid out of the tunnel. Sarah wondered if the sound of the engine had masked the crack of gunfire below and if Galley might now be lying dead in that dark tunnel.

Ned lit a smoke and chuckled. He took a few drags then flicked the smouldering butt at Wiley. It showered the old man's shirt with orange flames. Wiley glared at Ned. Ned started laughing, then stopped as he heard shouts from below.

Luke and Todd were in the gorge, calling up to him. 'Gawdamn,' Luke shouted, 'I never seen anything like it. He jumped the train, horse and all.'

Ned looked puzzled. 'What are ya yawkin about?'

Luke shook his head, as if in disbelief. 'He only got onto that train, Ned. Jumped his horse onto it. We thought we had him, too. Jesus.' He slapped his thigh in frustration. 'We had him so close.'

'So now what do we do?' Ned's good humour had left him.

'I don't like this,' Todd said nervously. 'A man does that, ain't no tellin' what he'll do. If I hadn't seen it with my own eyes, I would never believe it.' He shot a glance up the track, in the direction of the dwindling train. 'I say we git outta here before he comes back.'

'What about these two?' Ned asked, nodding at Wiley and Sarah.

'I say we leave 'em,' Todd said. 'I don't want no more to do with this.'

Luke thumped him on the shoulder and pointed a finger at his brother. 'This ain't finished. He made us look like fools at the Wheel and he's gonna pay. We got his friend and his woman. He's gonna come back all right, but this time we'll be waitin' and ready. We ain't far from Blue Water Creek. There's a place there where we can set a trap for him.' He grunted with satisfaction at his own plan and nodded. 'Ned, get the horses. We'll tie those two up and head for the creek.'

Ned turned back to Sarah and Wiley. He smiled. 'Looks like your friend's gonna wish he never crossed the Coltons.'

★ ★ ★

Galley's horse topped the rocky rise and he slid from his saddle, knelt on the ground and examined the brush and sparse grass among the rocks. He took a cursory glance at the gorge below and the railroad tunnel where he had been trapped only an hour ago. He found a cigarillo butt in the grass and held it to his nose. The butt was cold. Relighting it and drawing on the smoke, he surveyed the area.

Walking in concentric circles from the place he had found the butt, he widened his search of the ground. He found tracks in the dirt to the north. Five horses. Examining the pattern of the hoof marks, he noted that the two rear horses' tracks were a set distance behind the other three. Probably tied to the leading horses. Perhaps Sarah and Wiley were still alive.

Crouching in the dirt, Galley traced his finger around the crescent of one hoof mark. The Coltons had made a mistake: they had turned tail and were trying to get away from him.

And hunting men was what he was best at.

6

Yellow Bird stalked quietly through the forest. He wore the ceremonial robes of his people, the Lakota Sioux. To an observer, he might look as if he were stalking an animal as he moved gracefully through the trees. But he was not hunting today.

He was waiting for a sign.

He was a medicine man, as his father had been, and his father before him also. And as medicine man, he had been sent out here, into the pine forest, to find an answer to his tribe's current problem. A week ago, a white man with red hair had entered the mountains which the Sioux held sacred. He had brought two other men with him and they had been in the mountains ever since. This was very bad for the Lakota Sioux.

Because the mountains were not held

sacred for purely religious purposes; there was a very practical reason for the Sioux to fear the white men. If they found the secret of the mountains, white men would come from all over like a swarm of locusts and the area would be destroyed. The Sioux were scared. And they had sent their medicine man out to the forest to look for a sign to tell them what to do.

Yellow Bird had been out here for three days, eating little and drinking from a stream which emptied into Blue Water Creek a few miles away. He was tired and hungry and he hoped the Great Spirit would send him a sign soon so that he could return to the village and his people.

He stopped as he heard a branch crack in the forest to his right. He remained still, listening. He heard movement in the trees and the sound of something large crashing through the undergrowth toward him. His instincts told him to run for his life but he had been taught to overcome his fear and he remained where he was. He had no weapon; he was not allowed to carry one while on a vision quest. The crashing sound came closer. He heard an angry growl. It sounded close, too close.

The bear came lumbering out of the trees ahead of him. It reared up on its hind quarters and roared, displaying a vicious set of sharp teeth. Its muscles rippled beneath its white fur.

Its *white* fur.

When he saw the colour of the creature's pelt, Yellow Bird knew he was hallucinating. After three days in the forest, with little food, his mind was playing tricks on him. The skill of the medicine man, as his father and grandfather had taught him, was to interpret the vision which came to him while in this state.

The white bear dropped to all fours and glared at him. It huffed through its nose and turned, crashing away through the undergrowth.

Yellow Bird remained still, waiting to

see if the vision was over or if anything else would happen. He waited for twelve heartbeats. When nothing else occurred, he turned around and headed back to his village.

The sign had come. Yellow Bird was pleased. His people would be pleased also.

★   ★   ★

The Sioux village consisted of a huddle of buffalo hide teepees nestled beneath the mountains. As Yellow Bird walked out of the woods, he felt glad to be among his people again. They gathered around him, eagerly waiting to hear what he had to say.

Yellow Bird had interpreted his vision of the bear during his walk back to the village and he wondered if his people would like what he had to say. He knew that when he spoke to the Council, there would be many bad feelings. His interpretation of the vision would not be well received.

He entered the large teepee where the Council waited to hear him. The Council consisted of four members and Big Foot, the Sioux Chief. Of all the members, Yellow Bird knew that High Hawk, a headstrong warrior and leader of the Wolf Clan, would raise the most opposition to the medicine man's suggestion. High Hawk hated all white men with a passion and Yellow Bird's vision had told him that a white man would be coming to the village.

Big Foot gestured for Yellow Bird to sit before the Council. 'Tell us, Yellow Bird, has the Great Spirit spoken to you in the forest and told you how we can stop this flame-haired white man from finding the secret of our mountain?'

Yellow Bird nodded. 'I have been sent a sign.'

'And what did the sign say?' High Hawk asked. 'Should we continue to hunt and try to kill this white man?' A group of warriors had been sent into the mountains every day searching for the flame-haired one but had not managed to locate him.

Yellow Bird hesitated before answering High Hawk. Perhaps he had misread his vision of the bear. Perhaps he was wrong. No. He had been taught the way of the medicine man and he had used his skill to translate the vision of the white bear into an answer for his people. 'No,' he said. 'We cannot kill this flame-haired one. A white man will come. He will kill him.'

'A white man?' High Hawk shouted angrily. 'Our problem is a white man. How can we leave it up to another white man to solve it?'

Yellow Bird shrugged. 'I have been sent a vision of a white bear. A white man will come here. He is angry, like the bear, and he is ferocious like the bear. But his anger blinds him. We must help him and he will help us by using his skills to kill the flame-haired one who has violated our sacred mountain.'

High Hawk stood up angrily. 'Help the white man? The white man has brought us nothing but trouble. He has

an evil medicine which destroys everything he touches. He is taking our land.
He is trying to destroy the ways of our
ancestors. We fight the white man, we
do not help him!'

Yellow Bird had expected such a
reaction from the Wolf Clan leader.
High Hawk had once had a sister called
Silver Moon. She had been killed while
out riding, shot by a white man in a
passing train. Killed for no reason at all
other than someone else's amusement.

Big Foot gestured for High Hawk to
sit down. He thought for a moment.
'High Hawk speaks wisely,' he said.
'White man has brought us many
troubles. Tell me, Yellow Bird, why
should we trust this man who will come
like the bear?'

The medicine man hesitated again.
What he had to say next would anger
High Hawk even more. 'This man is
different from most of the white people.
He has strong medicine within him. But
he is fighting himself. These things the
Great Spirit has told me. Also, I have

been told how we can help this white man so that he will help us by killing the flame-haired one.'

'How?' Big Foot asked.

Yellow Bird looked at his Chief. 'He must dance the Ghost Dance,' he said.

All four members of the Council started shouting angrily. Yellow Bird had expected this reaction. But he was a medicine man. He had to tell his people the truth which the Great Spirit had imparted to him.

Big Foot shook his head. 'The Ghost Dance is a ceremony sacred to our people. No white man has ever taken part.'

'The Great Spirit says that this man must,' Yellow Bird said.

Big Foot looked at all the members of the Council. Every one looked angry at the medicine man's suggestion. High Hawk stared at Yellow Bird with open disgust. 'Yellow Bird, leave us now,' the Chief said. 'We will decide what to do about this white man who will come.'

'Will we allow him to take part in the

Ghost Dance?' the medicine man asked.

Big Foot sighed. 'The Council will discuss this matter further. High Hawk speaks wisely when he says that we should fight the white man. He has only brought us trouble and despair. You say this white man will come to us like an angry bear. Sometimes the only way to deal with such a creature is to kill it.'

7

Sarah felt exhausted. They had been riding for several hours and her muscles and bones ached. Her hands were tied behind her back and her horse was tied to the saddle of Todd Colton's mare.

Todd had a habit of glancing behind him nervously. He seemed to be watching the pine trees behind Sarah and he kept his hand close to his holstered gun. The fact that Galley had spooked Todd Colton pleased Sarah but also scared her. She was relieved that Galley had escaped Todd and Luke in the rail tunnel but she did not think he would be so lucky again; the Coltons would not underestimate him next time.

She turned to Wiley. He was beside her on his own horse, hands also tied. He looked much more frail than he had when they had set off and she wondered if he was mad at himself for not protecting her from the Coltons. He was an old man with bad joints but she supposed all men felt it their duty to protect women from the evils of the world; even old men who could not lift a gun any more.

He looked at her and smiled weakly. She smiled back. 'Do you suppose John's all right?' she whispered.

He nodded. 'From what those two said back at the gorge, he pulled a hell of a stunt getting onto that train.' He chuckled lightly. 'I knew he was good with horses but I never seen him do anything like that.'

'Do you think he'll come to help us?'

He nodded again. 'He'll be coming. His job is tracking down men and killing them. And he's damned good at his job.' He looked worried for a moment. 'Only I don't know what these yahoos have in mind. Maybe they're just blowin' smoke about setting a trap for John but after what they saw him do in that tunnel, I don't think they'd be provoking him none unless they thought they had a chance to get the drop on him.'

She stretched her aching muscles and winced as pain shot down her legs. 'I'll be glad when we get to Blue Water Creek so I can get off this horse,' she said.

'Shut up back there,' Luke Colton shouted over his shoulder.

'Maybe we should rest a while,' Ned suggested. 'Sun's starting to go down.'

Todd Colton looked panicked. 'No, we can't stop. He'll catch up with us. He'll kill us if we stop.' The blood had drained from his face and his eyes were wide.

'Stop your whining,' Luke growled. 'He ain't no spirit, he's just a man.'

'You saw the way he jumped his horse onto that train,' Todd said. 'Maybe he is just a man, but he's got some spirits watchin' over him.'

'Just horsemanship and luck,' Luke said.

'Ain't no one got that much luck.'

'He's just a man. He can be shot like anyone else.'

'And he had four aces at the Lucky Wheel. Jesus.' Todd whirled around and stared wide-eyed at the trees behind them as if he expected Galley to come swooping down on them, guns blazing.

'When we get to the creek, I'll show ya how easy he is to kill,' Luke said.

'Shut up, both of ya,' Ned snorted. 'He'll find us for sure if you keep arguing and whining like the fools you are.'

Luke shook his head. 'He can't be caught up with us yet. He's gotta get off that train first.'

'That won't be no problem for him,' Todd said. 'You saw how easy he got on it.'

'And then he's gotta pick up our trail,' Luke went on.

'That'll be easy,' Todd said. 'We got five horses. A blind man could follow our trail.'

'That's the point. We want him to

86

find us and walk into our trap at the creek.'

'Unless he finds us before we get to the creek.' Todd still stared at the trees around them. 'I'm tellin' ya, that guy ain't normal.'

'Stop talking like that,' Ned said. 'You're makin' me damn nervous.'

'Four aces,' Todd whispered. 'Four aces.'

★　★　★

The forests thinned out and then gave way to prairie. By the time they were nearing Blue Water Creek, the sun was no longer visible. The evening sky was heavy with dark clouds and the air felt charged, as if a storm were coming. Luke Colton looked up at the sky and said, 'It's gonna rain some. Those clouds are thunderheads.'

Ned nodded. 'It'll cover our trail. Perhaps he won't be able to find us.'

'He'll find us,' Todd said. He had calmed down since leaving the forest behind but his eyes still darted nervously around and he constantly stroked the butt of his gun with his thumb. 'What's your plan, Luke?'

'It's a little further yet,' Luke said.

They rode across the prairie while the thunderheads rolled and darkened in the sky.

Luke stopped as they came to the bank of a fast-flowing river. 'North Platte River,' he said, staring into the deep water. 'Can't take a horse across it. Too deep and too wide. Only way across is a cattle bridge half a mile downriver, near Blue Water Creek. That's where we'll get him.' He spurred his horse along the riverbank, riding parallel to the deep water.

Sarah knew the bridge Luke was speaking of. She and her father had used it many times when moving cattle from their ranch north of Blue Water Creek to the railroad stations in the south. It was the only way to get across the river. The next bridge was four or five miles away. Galley would have to use this bridge to continue following their trail. On the opposite bank, where Blue Water Creek started, pine trees and scrub bushes dotted the prairie. She supposed Luke's plan must be to hide in those trees and shoot at Galley as he crossed the bridge. It was a simple plan but effective. Galley would be an easy target exposed on the cattle bridge.

They reached the wide wooden bridge and Luke pointed to it. 'When he comes over here,' he said, 'we'll be in those trees and we'll take him out. He's got no cover and we got plenty.'

'I don't know,' Todd said, shaking his head. 'What if we miss?'

'Miss? We'll be shooting from three angles. He'll be exposed on the bridge. If you could miss that, you ain't no brother of mine.'

'Ned missed him at the gorge.'

Ned scowled at Todd. 'The angles was all wrong. There ain't no way we can miss him this time.' Thunder rumbled in the dark sky. Ned looked up. 'We'd better get to some shelter in those trees. Ain't no tellin' when he'll get here.'

They crossed the bridge and dismounted. 'Take them two into the creek a ways,' Luke said to Ned. 'Tie 'em to a tree and tie their mouths up. I don't want 'em warning him.'

Ned led all the horses along the creek, his boots splashing in the shallow, murky water. He found a secluded spot among some trees and tethered the horses. 'Get down,' he said to Sarah and Wiley.

Sarah slid from her saddle and felt the blood run back into her dead legs. Ned sat her and Wiley down on a patch of dirt near a solid tree and took some rope from his saddle bag. He wrapped the rope around them, clinching it tight around the trunk of the tree. Sarah struggled but the rope was tight and cut into her arms if she moved too much.

Ned took a piece of rope and used his knife to cut it into two smaller pieces. He tied these around Sarah's and Wiley's mouths. 'There,' he said, examining his handiwork. 'At least you won't get too wet here. Trees'll keep most of the rain off.' He turned away and went to rejoin his brothers as they waited for Galley.

Thunder rolled and it began to rain.

* * *

As he reached the edge of the woods and the beginning of the prairie, John Galley cursed. He had been following the Coltons' trail for hours through the forest and now he had two problems; the weather and the terrain.

Because of the rain, which was starting to come down heavily, he wasn't sure how old the trail was. The Colton brothers might be miles ahead or might have passed this spot just a few minutes ago. He had no way of knowing now that the rain had started.

His second problem was the prairie. There was no cover. If the Coltons were near, they would spot him coming out of the trees and they would know he was following them. He would be an easy target in open landscape

He drew his horse back under cover of the pines. His saddlebag contained a poncho covered with waterproof oil. Galley slipped it on and debated his next move. He knew that the Coltons must have crossed the bridge downriver. He would have to cross it himself to follow them. He could not ford the North Platte; it was too deep and fast.

Finally, he decided to head downriver but to stay within the cover of the trees until he got to the bridge. Once he got there, he had no choice and would have to break cover to get across the river.

He pulled on the reins and led his horse through the trees as the rain lashed down and lightning flashed in the distance.

★ ★ ★

Todd Colton's hands shook as he held the Winchester rifle. It wasn't only cold that made them shake, although he was wet and cold as he hid behind the brush at the edge of the creek. His hands shook mostly with fear.

He knew it wasn't rational. Galley was outnumbered three to one and they had him for sure when he came over the bridge. Even in this damned rain and lightning, they couldn't miss such an easy target. Galley was as good as dead.

Yet still Todd was afraid.

Because Galley had been as good as dead once before, maybe even twice if you counted the time Luke had held the derringer in his face at the Lucky Wheel, and both times he had survived.

That was more than luck.

Todd believed in omens. His mother was a highly superstitious woman and, although none of her beliefs had rubbed off on Ned or Luke, Todd put a lot of stock by such things as dreams and portents.

Galley had drawn four aces.

He had looked down the barrel of

Luke's derringer and was still alive to tell the tale.

He had been trapped in the rail tunnel, no way out.

But he had found a way out.

Todd wished Ned and Luke hadn't been so stubborn about getting revenge on Galley. Sometimes, you had to know when to cut your losses. Todd wanted nothing more to do with this. Yet here he was, gun in hand, ready to help his brothers kill Galley.

Try to kill Galley.

He pushed that thought from his mind.

He watched the bridge closely. The river was swelling now as the storm raged angrily. Galley would have to cross over the bridge and they would shoot him. Simple. Todd swallowed hard. It sounded simple and if it had been any other man, Todd would have been confident of success. But Galley was different from most men. He seemed to be driven by something. Where most men would have given up, he took control of the situation and fought on.

Lightning flashed.

Todd tried to stop his hands shaking. He watched the dark woods on the far side of the river. He imagined John Galley somewhere in those woods, coming after them, angry because of what had happened at the gorge.

Lightning arced across the sky and Todd jumped. He had to stop spooking himself. Luke was right; Galley was just a man. He could be shot like anyone else.

Todd watched the dark woods and his hands shook worse than before.

★ ★ ★

Galley squinted through the dark and rain and could just make out the bridge. The sky was growing blacker by the minute. He would have to break cover now to get over the river, then into the creek on the far side. He wondered momentarily if the Coltons might have laid a trap at the bridge. It was a good place to catch a man out, exposed on that bridge. Galley squinted at the trees and brush on the far side of the river but the growing darkness covered everything.

Still, he did not move out of the cover of the pines. It could be a trap. Was this where it would all end, on a bridge near the mountains? He supposed it was as good a place as any. He thought of all the people he had killed, their faces etched clearly in his mind.

He had nearly been killed himself a couple of times. Bill Holmes had almost got him with his trap. Would the Coltons succeed where all others had failed?

An unbidden memory came into his head and he remembered a time long ago when he had been tracking three other brothers. Those three had also tried to kill him. He pushed the painful memory away.

He looked at the darkening pines

around him. He had no choice. The bridge waited.

★ ★ ★

Todd glanced to his left and saw Luke hunkered behind a small tree. Beyond Luke, Ned lay on his stomach behind a patch of scrub. His Winchester was propped on the trunk of a nearby pine. Luke held two Smith & Wessons. He took a quick peek from behind his tree then ducked down. 'He's coming,' he warned.

Todd felt his stomach tighten. He risked a glance through the brush but saw nothing on the dark plain. He squinted but still saw nothing. Perhaps Luke had been mistaken.

But then lightning flashed, illuminating the prairie with a ghostly light, and Todd saw the figure. He rode cautiously out of the trees across the river. He wore a poncho, and in the dark, all Todd could make out was a black shape upon a horse. Like the Grim Reaper.

His hand trembled faster. He told himself to calm down.

He turned away for a moment because he couldn't bear to look at that shape, slightly darker than the surrounding prairie, riding toward him.

Then he turned back because he had to be ready to fire as soon as Galley reached the bridge.

Galley was almost there now. Todd turned toward Luke, who was cocking his Smith & Wessons. Beyond, his other brother was aiming the Winchester at the dark rider.

He turned back just as Galley's horse stepped onto the bridge. Lightning flashed and for a moment, the bridge was starkly illuminated. He heard a crack as Luke opened fire, then another as Ned fired the Winchester. He took aim and squeezed the trigger of his own rifle.

The horse on the bridge reared up and flailed at the air with its hooves. The rider fell from its back and toppled into the river. 'Got the sonuvabitch,'

Luke shouted, standing up and walking toward the river. The horse fled back the way it had come, back to the dark trees. Todd left the cover of the brush and joined Luke and Ned.

They'd killed the bastard!

Luke was right after all. Galley did not lead a charmed life; he was just a man and bullets could kill him like any other man. The three brothers walked to the swollen river's edge.

Galley lay face down in the water, his poncho rippling with the current of the river. Luke slid down the muddy bank toward the body. He was laughing. 'Got ya, you bastard. Came right into my trap.' He turned to Ned. 'Pass me your rifle.'

Ned passed him the Winchester and Luke prodded the body with the stock. Galley had to be dead; there was no way they had missed him. Todd felt his fear lift.

Luke prodded the body harder. The poncho rolled over and Todd felt his blood run cold.

The poncho was full of pine branches.

'Jesus,' Luke shouted. 'It ain't him.' He stumbled back onto the slippery river bank with surprise, his face a mask of panic.

Then everything happened at once.

The murky water near Luke sprayed everywhere as a figure burst from the river. Galley looked like a river demon. His hair was plastered to his face and he was soaked with muddy river water. His eyes seemed to be on fire, burning with anger. Lightning flashed as Galley lunged at Luke. Luke actually screamed. Todd had never heard his brother scream before but he was screaming now as Galley went for him. Something flashed in Galley's hand and Todd realised he had a knife. Luke cried out and went down hard, falling into the cold river, his screams cut off.

But Todd could not shoot. His hands were shaking uncontrollably. If he needed any proof that this man was charmed, he had it now. Galley had second-guessed them and avoided their trap, sending his horse and poncho to the bridge while he swam there from a point further upriver.

Luke was dead. Ned was unarmed. Todd was too scared to shoot.

Galley held all the aces.

Todd threw the rifle at Ned and ran. He saw Ned grab at the rifle stock, but too late. By the time he had a grip on the gun, Galley was on him, the knife flashing again. Todd ran in blind panic through the storm, expecting to feel the cold steel of the knife cutting into him from behind.

He stumbled blindly into the creek and the cold water splashed around him. He ran without looking back because he knew that if he did, he would see Galley coming after him, the bloody knife slashing the air in front of his demonic face. He ran and ran until his legs finally gave out and he collapsed to the ground, cold, wet and scared.

He lay on the ground shivering with

cold and fright and he waited for Galley to come and find him. After a few moments, he imagined that he saw ghostly shapes moving through the storm-swept trees. Then he realised that he wasn't imagining the shapes at all; they were real. Then he realised that they were Indians and he started screaming.

8

As he stumbled along the river's edge, holding the knife loosely, Galley felt as if he were encased in a block of ice. His fingers and toes were numb and that numbness was slowly creeping up his arms and legs. The river had been deathly cold.

He squinted through the lashing rain for the third Colton brother but the night was too dark and the weather too severe for him to see anything more than a few trees and bushes. Some of the dark shapes *could* be a man crouching low, waiting to fire at him, but he was sure the third brother had fled into the creek.

Shivering uncontrollably, he wondered if swimming in the cold waters had been sensible. Sure, he was alive, but for how long? He felt the numbness reach his shoulders and knees, seeping into his joints like liquid ice and stiffening them. He had to find Wiley and Sarah quickly.

He stumbled into the creek and a tangle of low, sharp branches cut him. He saw the long cuts on his hands but could not feel them. Splashing through the water he began to panic. What if his body froze and stiffened and he collapsed here, left to die in the cold creek water? Death, of course, didn't worry him but he hadn't found Wiley or Sarah yet. He refused to die until he knew they were safe.

His arms and legs began to lock up as the chill swept through them. It spread faster now and he knew it would soon have him completely in its icy grip.

Maybe now I die.

No.

He plunged blindly through the dark creek, desperate to find his friends. He thought for a moment that he had been wrong all along and the Coltons had killed Sarah and Wiley back at the gorge. His manhunt had been simple revenge and not a rescue at all. If that was the case, he could die here in this creek and it wouldn't matter. He could lie down and let the cold wash over him, slowly drawing the life from him. He would forget about the cabin in Canada and Emma Holt forever.

No. He had to believe that Sarah and Wiley were still alive. He had to keep looking. Lightning flashed and he saw a shape that might be a horse a little way ahead of him. He headed for it and lightning flashed again. It was a horse.

Galley weaved toward it. His legs felt disconnected from the rest of his body. He reached the animal and found four others tethered alongside it. A few feet away, Sarah and Wiley were tied to a tree.

Sarah spotted him and shrunk back, her eyes wide with terror. Galley realised he must look frightening; he was plastered with mud and blood and his cold-stiffened movements were unnatural.

He stumbled toward Sarah and fell to his knees. He felt for the rope with numb fingers and started sawing at it with his knife. It snapped. His vision blurred. The effort had been too much for him.

Shapes appeared in his vision, then pinpricks of white light.

Then darkness.

* * *

Sarah managed to struggle out of her ropes and remove the gag from her mouth. She bent over Galley's body fearful that he might be dead. He looked awful. The skin of his face and hand was blue and his body felt like ice when she touched him. She felt a small flicker of relief when she saw his chest rising and falling with his shallow breaths. He wasn't dead. Yet.

She looked over at Wiley, who was struggling to his feet, and said, 'We've got to get him somewhere warm. The ranch house isn't far from here. Let's get him on one of these horses.'

They heaved the cold, unmoving body over to the horses. Wiley grunted with the effort and Sarah knew that the old man's joints must be aching from the wet and the cold. They lay Galley down near the hooves of Luke Colton's horse. 'Whaddya reckon happened to him?' Wiley asked.

She shrugged. 'He must have killed the Coltons but it looks like he fell into the river. We've got to get him dry and warm fast.'

She took Galley's arms and Wiley grabbed the legs and they heaved him up onto the saddle. His body lay draped across it on his stomach, river water dripping from him. Sarah grabbed the rope which had tied them earlier and set about securing Galley to the saddle.

Wiley leaned heavily against a tree, catching his breath. Sarah felt concern for the old man. He looked bad. He was too old to be out here in this weather. 'You OK, Wiley?' she asked him.

He held up a hand and looked at her,

wheezing. 'Just let me get my breath back. I ain't as young as I used to be. There was once a day when I would've handled those Coltons all by myself. Not any more, though. I guess my fightin' days are over.'

He untethered the horses and climbed onto Ned Colton's mount. Sarah swung her leg over Todd Colton's pinto and they set off through the creek, hers and Wiley's horses still tied behind the Coltons'.

'We've got to head north to reach the ranch,' Sarah said. They followed the creek for a while and eventually, the storm eased off some. The rain still came down angrily but the lightning passed. Sarah glanced at Galley, worried that he might slip off the saddle, but the rope held his body securely.

As they rode north, the mountains reaching proudly ahead of them, Sarah realised that Wiley was close to dropping from his own saddle. His old body swayed erratically with his horse's movements and he leaned over to the left. He hadn't spoken a word since they had set off for the ranch house, and Sarah wondered if he was ill. His body was too old for this. At his age, he should be taking his days easy, not riding around Dakota in a downpour.

She leaned over to him. 'You OK, Wiley?'

He looked at her and his eyes, behind his rain-streaked glasses, were dull and confused. He didn't seem to recognise her. Still, he smiled slightly.

They rode in silence the only sound the hissing of the rain and distant thunder, until the ranch house came into view.

The sight of the house made Sarah feel both relieved and sad. Relieved because she could get Galley and Wiley warm and dry. Sad because it made her think of her father lying dead some-where in those imposing mountains, killed by that bastard Red McCready.

She rode to the stables and slid from her saddle. Wiley stayed mounted. Sarah walked over to him. 'Wiley,' she said, touching his leg. 'We're at the ranch house.'

Wiley slipped from the saddle, dead. He lay on the ground, the rain coating his glasses so she could not see his unseeing eyes. The cold, the wet, and the stress he had been put under had killed the old man. He had died quietly during the ride from the creek.

Sarah dragged Wiley's frail body into the stables, out of the rain. She would tend to it later, but right now she had to deal with the still-living. She walked over to Galley and started to untie him. Then a cold thought crossed her mind and she hesitated. When she loosened the rope, would Galley slip from the saddle dead as well? Had he also succumbed to the embrace of the Reaper?

Laying a hand on his soaked shirt, she felt a flutter of a heartbeat. He was still alive. She untied him quickly.

She dragged him across to the house, his boot heels leaving twin furrows in the wet dirt, and up onto the porch.

The wood was scarred where Red McCready had shot it.

A sudden panic washed through her.

What if Red was in the house? What if, after killing her father and driving her off, he had taken to living there?

No, the house was dark. If Red were living here, he would have some lamps lit inside.

Wouldn't he?

She had left the Remington with the horses, and Galley seemed to have lost his gun before turning up at the creek. He had been carrying a knife, though, and she had slipped it into his belt before strapping him to the horse. She retrieved it and pushed open the ranch house door.

The hallway beyond was dark and quiet. Leaving Galley on the porch, she stepped into the darkness, the knife held tightly in front of her, shaking slightly with the trembling of her hand. She half-expected a rush of movement from the shadows, Red McCready leaping out at her, but all was quiet.

She moved to the kitchen, trying to be quiet as she stepped along the floorboards. Apart from the stove and table, the kitchen was empty. The two bedrooms and sitting room were empty too, and she finally went back to the porch to fetch Galley.

Straining, she dragged him to her father's bedroom and peeled off his wet clothes. She rummaged through her father's wardrobe and found one of his woollen shirts. She slipped it over Galley's shoulders and laid him in the bed, pulling the blankets up to his chin in an effort to get him warm.

She went to the kitchen and lit the stove to warm up the house, then returned to the stables. Unsaddling the five horses and getting them fixed up with hay and water took a lot of time and effort. By the time she was done, she was exhausted. Still, she had one more task to tend to before she went back to the house.

Grabbing a shovel from the stable wall, she set out into the gentle rain to find a suitable place to set Wiley to rest. She settled on a spot near the mountains and set to digging.

She was dripping with sweat by the time the hole was deep enough. She dragged Wiley from the stables and buried him in the shadow of the mountains. Although she hadn't known the old man long, she felt a sadness at his passing. She found some wood in the stables and fashioned a crude cross. Setting the grave marker into the dirt, she wondered how Galley would react to the death of his friend.

If Galley ever gets better, she told herself.

Quietly, she said a short prayer over Wiley's grave.

She turned back to the house, then stopped. She looked up at the dark mountains and a wave of fear washed through her. She supposed it was the sight of the mountains again. Once, she had loved them and could spend hours watching them, marvelling at the way the sun and clouds made shadows move across them, bringing the mountains to life. Now, the sight of them made a deep sadness fill her heart.

It wasn't until later, when she was lying in her bed, listening to the rain drumming on the roof, that she realised the fear she had felt hadn't been because of the sight of the mountains.

She had been afraid because she had felt like she was being watched.

9

The following morning, the sun rose like a golden orb above the mountains. All signs of last night's storm were gone. The day was warm and dry, the sky clear blue. Sarah made a breakfast of pancakes. As they sizzled on the skillet, she stared out of the window at the mountains again. Again, she felt as if someone was hiding out there and watching her. The thought sent a shiver of fear up her back. She squinted against the sunlight but could see no one out there.

She went to Galley's room and opened the door. He was still asleep but tossing about slightly, as if dreaming. Sarah closed the door again, thankful that the bounty hunter was still alive. She returned to the kitchen. She would make some breakfast for Galley after she had eaten her own. She was famished. Yesterday's events had taken their toll on her. Her stomach rumbled emptily as she slid her pancakes from the skillet to her plate. She had taken her first bite when the shout came from Galley's room.

Leaving her breakfast, she rushed to his bedside. He was moaning in a low, keening voice. Although he had been cold last night, he was sweating now. Sarah felt his forehead. He was burning up. Some sort of fever had taken hold of him.

She shook his shoulders lightly. 'John,' she said. 'It's Sarah. Wake up! You're having a nightmare.'

His eyes remained closed and he shook his head back and forth. 'No,' he whispered. 'No.' He continued to writhe in her arms.

'John, wake up.' she said, shaking him.

Suddenly, his eyes flew open and stared at her. They were bloodshot. 'I killed her,' he shouted. 'I killed her!'

'Who?'

But he had fallen back to the pillows and resumed his nightmare. He was in the grip of a fever dream.

Sarah went out to the back of the house to draw water from the well her father had built. As she did so, she again felt uneasy. Someone was out here, she was sure of it.

She rushed back inside and took a glass of water to Galley. He was thrashing around too violently for her to get him to drink it, so she dipped a cloth into the cold liquid and gently applied it to his hot brow.

As she tended to him, she realised that even though she hardly knew him, she cared deeply for John Galley. He had come to rescue her and Wiley from the Coltons. He was going to help her avenge her father. He was a good man. She felt hot, stinging tears roll down her cheeks. She cried for her father, dead in the mountains. She cried for Wiley Jones, buried out back. She cried for John Galley, twisted by some dark secret past.

And she cried for herself because she understood that she loved a man who hated himself. If only she could show him that he did not deserve this self-punishment. If only she could teach him to love himself as she loved him. But she knew that was impossible. Any dreams she built involving John Galley were like castles made of sand and would be washed away by the dark tide of his memories.

He stopped his thrashing about and lay on his back, his chest rising and falling heavily. He whispered something but Sarah could not make out what he said.

She wiped the sweat from his forehead. He whispered the word again.

She leaned closer to his face, feeling his hot breath on her cheek. 'What did you say, John?' she asked him.

He whispered the word again. 'Emma.'

Wiley had said that John talked in his sleep. It seemed that during sleep, he re-lived his secret past. That was happening now and Sarah wished she could get inside his head to see what was troubling him. She desperately wanted to help.

He whispered 'Emma' again and Sarah wondered what feverish dreams were haunting him. Surely no man deserved the life John Galley seemed to lead; hounded by memories he could not escape but could only destroy by destroying himself.

Her own helplessness frustrated her. Unless she knew what demons lurked in his skull, she could not help Galley. She could only watch as he rode down the road to oblivion.

'Emma,' he whispered again.

Sarah watched him as he dreamed his dark dreams.

10

John Galley watched with wonder as Emma came through the woods, her arms filled with wildflowers. They created a splash of vivid colour against his wife's white blouse. Her long blue skirt undulated around her legs as the warm breeze blew it, making it seem like a wavy blue ocean. She was smiling. She had never stopped smiling since they had arrived in Canada three months ago, the dark, dirty streets of London behind them, to be replaced by the virgin forests of this new land.

She sat beside him on the ground and showed him her colourful prizes.

He shook his head and smiled. 'There are more flowers in our cabin than in the woods.'

Laughing, she poked him in the ribs. 'I have to brighten up the place somehow. There's only one window and it's too dull.'

'The house'll be done soon,' he replied. The cabin, sitting in the woods near the Ottawa River, was only temporary while John and a bunch of local settlers built stronger houses further downriver. A small town was springing up there and John and Emma would have a house on the main street. 'We'll be living there soon, in the town,' he said.

'I don't mind it here,' she said quickly. Perhaps too quickly. She knew that all his life, John's parents had believed their son would amount to nothing. They never said so openly but it was clearly implied by their disapproving looks and words. Nothing he did was good enough for them.

He had worked hard in London as a tailor and made a good living but his parents had looked down on that profession because John had not followed in his father's footsteps and become a watchmaker. His father had lined up John's apprenticeship at the shop where he worked but John had refused it and gone his own way.

He had married Emma Holt and they had disapproved of that because she was just a barmaid at the *Lion's Head*.

And when he had said he was taking Emma to Canada, to broaden his horizons and seek a new life in the New World, they had disapproved of that as well because he was leaving *them*, his loving parents, behind.

Emma knew of his parents' attempts to shatter his dreams and she never complained about their small, sometimes cold, cabin. Or the mosquitoes which felt like they were eating you alive come the dusk. Or the fact that there was no one around for miles. Her job at the *Lion's Head* had made her used to company and laughter but she did not complain that she now lived in a quiet wood where the company consisted of animals and the laughter

122

was heard by no one except the silent trees.

The solitude had brought them together. They had been close in London but out here in the wilds, they were connected in a way no city-dweller would ever understand. Emma seemed genuinely happy to be living in Canada and that made John ecstatic. His every move was designed to make her happy. She had changed a lot from the shy girl behind the bar at the *Lion's Head* whom he had fallen for the first time he laid eyes on her. She was now even more lovely. She believed in him when no one else would and that meant more to him than anything.

'Look, a raccoon,' she said, dropping the flowers into his lap and going into the cabin for bread. She loved nature, something John had never known until they had landed on these shores. The wildflowers, filling the cabin with their sweet fragrance, were a testimony to that.

John watched as the raccoon advanced

nervously into the clearing near the cabin. The animal's nose twitched as he breathed in the unfamiliar scent of man. His eyes shone from within his black bandit's mask.

'We'll feed you in a minute, fella,' John told the animal. 'You're lucky you dropped by.'

When Emma came back with the bread and tried to coax the raccoon to her, John watched her, realising how lucky he was to have such a wife. There were a few men, local settlers, who were alone here in Canada and John could not bear to think how deep that loneliness must be. To be in a strange country, on the brink of a new life, and not have someone to share all these new experiences with.

He watched Emma, crouching in the sunlight and throwing flakes of bread to the raccoon, and he was surprised when he felt a tear spill from his eye and course down his cheek. He didn't know why he had cried. He supposed his love for his wife had overwhelmed him for a minute there.

He did not know that he would be spilling many more tears, and a lot of blood, when the winter came.

★ ★ ★

Sarah sat on the edge of the bed and wiped the sweat from Galley's forehead, using the damp cloth. He was still now, but mumbling to himself. And his eyes were flickering and rolling relentlessly behind his closed lids.

He whispered something again. She missed it because he had hissed it out but it had not been 'Emma' again.

He hissed again. Two syllables. His voice was tremulous.

Sarah leaned close to his mouth. He whispered again.

'Winter,' he hissed. 'Winter.'

★ ★ ★

The snows came suddenly and blanketed everything with a sparkling, glassy

whiteness. The woods were transformed. The maples were now bare and
looked like old men's fingers pointing
to the snow-filled grey sky. The pines
became weighed down under their
heavy white covering and branches
drooped. Most of the animals disappeared, to dream away the cold time,
but the ones that did not hibernate
changed, their pelts growing thicker to
insulate them from the harsh winds.

The Galleys had also changed. John
had become thicker, more muscular.
When they had arrived in Canada, he
had weighed a hundred and forty
pounds but he was now pushing a
hundred and sixty, and most of it was
solid muscle. His hands, once fragile-
looking tailor's hands, were tough and
calloused. He could never become a
watch-maker like his father now. Those
hands were used to handling logs and
rocks, not delicate watch movements.

Emma had put on some weight as
well but it wasn't muscle. It was their
child. She had become pregnant in the

fall and was now three months into her term. They were both delighted. The house was almost finished and their child was on the way. Things were getting better all the time and John had written to his parents to tell them of their grandchild, Emma's job at the local school teaching the children to read and write, and their new house in the growing town.

He was sure his parents would read the letter, look at each other, shrug, and agree that their son had come to nothing, as they had always known he would.

He was building a crib for the baby when Emma came into the cabin, her face white and worried. He saw her expression and dropped his tools. He sat her down at their small table and held her hands in his. 'What is it, love?'

She looked at him and he saw tears welling in her large eyes. 'I . . . I've just been downriver, picking flowers, and . . . ' She brought her hands to her face and wept. He held her gently, upset even though he didn't know what had upset her.

'Tell me what's the matter, love,' he coaxed.

Her shoulders hitched a couple of times as she tried to stop her sobs. 'Someone's . . . someone's been killing the animals. The riverbank is littered with . . . carcasses.' The tears came again and John held her tightly, his own tears hot on his cheeks. He couldn't bear to see Emma upset.

'Is it trappers?' he asked.

She shook her head. 'I don't know, John.'

He got up and pulled on his heavy coat. Grabbing his rifle from the wall, he said, 'Where?'

'A little downriver,' she replied through her tears. 'You can't miss it.' She saw the rifle and added. 'For God's sake, John, be careful.'

He nodded and stepped out into the cold winter wind. The evening was fast approaching and the sky hung heavy with more snow. He felt the wind dry his tears, leaving cold tracks down his cheeks where they had once been. He set off downriver, trudging through the deep snow, the rifle loaded.

* * *

He was thrashing back and forth on the bed now and sweat covered his fevered body. Sarah felt an urge to throw off the covers and cool his burning body but she knew that was wrong. The best way to get rid of a fever was to sweat it out.

Galley started moaning and shaking.

Sarah left him to get more water. She drew the liquid from the well and slaked her own thirst. The day was hot. She shaded her eyes and peered at the mountains behind the ranch. They looked majestic, rising proudly into the blue sky, and again Sarah felt the stab of a double-edged sword of emotion. Happy because the mountains were glorious. Sad because her father was dead somewhere among those rocks.

Soon, perhaps, Red McCready would

be dead for that. If Galley got well again. *Of course he will*, she told herself. *He's fit and strong. A fever won't kill him.*

Unless he lets it.

That thought worried her and she hurried back to the ranch house. She got to the porch, then stopped. Had she seen a flash of movement near the mountains?

She shaded her eyes again and stared hard at the place where she thought it had been. Nothing moved. There wasn't even a breeze to stir the grass. She was sure she had seen something, though. It must be her eyes playing tricks on her. Still, that feeling of being watched washed over her and she felt the hairs on the back of her neck prickle and stand up. *Stop being foolish*, she chastised herself. Even so, when she got back to the kitchen, she locked the door and took the Remington with her back to Galley's room.

He was lying still and her first thought was, *Oh God. He's let it take him*. But he was breathing shallowly. As she placed the water by the bedside, he uttered a new word. 'Trappers,' he intoned.

Sarah wiped his forehead with the cool water. 'Trappers,' he whispered. He said the word as if it held some talismanic power. As if it explained everything.

★ ★ ★

There were three of them. John found their tracks in the snow, leading away from the slaughter by the river's edge. They were wearing snowshoes and the round impressions in the fresh snow were easy for him to follow.

They had skinned all manner of animals by the river and left the carcasses there to rot. John had found the place easily. A number of carrion birds were flocking to the area, cawing loudly in delight at this bloody treat that man had left for them.

It was almost dark when he found

them. He had been following the snowshoe impressions for nearly an hour, heading deeper into the forest, when he saw the glimmer of a campfire through the trees. Moving through the trees toward it, he clutched the rifle tightly, angrily.

The dusk light made strange shadows beneath the trees. The snow seemed to glow with a ghostly whiteness. John crept through the shadows until he could hear voices. They were laughing and joking but the language was strange and alien to John. He pressed himself behind a Douglas fir and peered toward the camp.

The three men were sitting on a fallen log, wearing furs. Bearded and dark-haired, their family resemblance was remarkable. Their gnarled features, revealed in the flickering firelight, were almost identical. Hooked noses. Black beady eyes. They were eating cooked meat and had pitched a small tent in the snow behind them. Their traps were piled behind the tent, steel jaws dripping with melted snow. Their guns and snowshoes were leaning against another fallen log near the tent. Out of reach.

John stepped forward out of cover of the trees and the three men looked at him, startled. Then, as they saw that he was alone, they relaxed visibly. The man sitting between his two brothers looked around at the guns lying near the snowshoes, then looked back as John lifted his rifle.

The man smiled. His mouth was slick with grease from his meat. '*Bonjour, monsieur*,' he said.

They were French-Canadian, John realised, probably from Quebec. He said, 'Any of you speak English?'

The man on the left nodded. 'Yes,' he said, his eyes fixed on John's rifle barrel, his accent thick. 'Allow me to introduce us. I am Jacques Delatoire and these is my brothers. Alain *et* Jean-Pierre.' At the mention of their names, the other two nodded.

'You responsible for that God-awful

mess at the river?' John asked.

Jacques smiled and shrugged. '*Oui, monsieur*. It is a regrettable part of our business.'

John felt a sickness rise within him. These men killed without feeling. They raped the land without a second thought. All in the name of money. 'I want you to take your business off my land,' he said.

Jacques shook his head. 'But we are not yet finished here.'

John brought his rifle around so that it pointed directly at the trapper's face. 'Yes you are.'

The three brothers looked at each other and it seemed to John as if some unspoken communication passed between them. Jacques turned to him and said, almost ingratiatingly, '*Oui, Monsieur*, we will move on in the morning. Perhaps you would join us for coffee?' He held out a mug of steaming coffee to John. John knocked it out of the man's hand. The dark coffee stained the snow near the fire and the mug smashed on the ground.

'Just move on in the morning,' he said.

He backed toward the trees, keeping his rifle trained on the three trappers who watched him, all smiling savagely. He realised then that they would not leave his land in the morning. They had been cooperative only because he had held the rifle on them. They were like jackals, these men, bowing their heads and asking for mercy when threatened but striking out without any thought of such mercy when they held the upper hand. John knew he was going to have trouble from them.

He kept his rifle on them until they were out of sight behind the trees and then he ran. Perhaps they would come after him with their guns, killing him with no more remorse than they showed toward the animals they captured in their steel traps. John followed his own tracks back through the woods, feeling dangerously threatened. He glanced back occasionally but no one followed him through the snow.

When he got to the cabin, he was gasping, his breathing vaporising in the cold air. He waited before going inside. He wanted to catch his breath and calm down. Emma was distressed enough without knowing that he was afraid as well. He composed himself and went inside.

Emma was sitting at the table, her face anxious. John felt a flood of love for her as he saw that worried look. 'Oh, John, I was so worried about you,' she said as she came to him.

He took her in his arms and held her tight. 'I'm OK.'

'Did you find anyone?'

He nodded. 'Trappers. They said they'd leave in the morning.'

'Do you think they will?'

No, he thought. 'Yes,' he said.

She squeezed him tighter and rested her head on his shoulder. He watched the night black out the woods beyond the window. He wouldn't get much sleep tonight.

He would be too busy waiting for trouble.

⋆ ⋆ ⋆

The flicker of movement at the ranch house window startled Sarah. She had seen it out of the corner of her eye; a flash of colour in the periphery of her vision. She sprang off the bed and grabbed the Remington, leaning against the bedroom wall. The rifle shook in her trembling hands.

Someone was out there.

Red McCready? Had he somehow sensed that she was back in the house and come to kill her?

For one insane moment, her mind told her that maybe Wiley Jones had been at the window. Perhaps he had dug himself out of the shallow grave out back and come shambling to the house, intent on killing her and Galley for taking him with them on the ride that finally finished him. She tried to calm herself, tell herself she was acting like a frightened schoolgirl. But someone was out there. The feelings of being watched she had experienced at the well were real. Someone had definitely been at the window.

Galley shook slightly. His fevered sleep made him unaware of the danger outside, protected him from the fear that almost paralysed Sarah. But perhaps his fevered dreams held even greater fears for him.

Her knees weak, Sarah edged along the wall to the window, craning her neck to see outside without exposing herself. The land beyond the house seemed deserted.

She turned back to Galley, who was shaking and sweating. His eyes opened momentarily and he stared at the ceiling, his body still. He seemed awake. Sarah went to him and sat on the bed, the rifle on her lap. Galley seemed not to notice her. 'John,' she said, gently shaking him. 'Are you awake?'

'Danger,' he said, still staring unwaveringly at the ceiling.

'John?'

'Danger.' His eyes closed again.

She heard a thump on the roof. Her breath whooshed out of her and her body trembled with returning fear. Someone was on the Goddamned roof! She got up and fled from the room. She had to get out of the house now.

By the time she got to the kitchen, she knew she could not run. Galley was here. She could not leave him. It was unthinkable. No matter what danger threatened, she could not leave Galley. Scrabbling sounds came from the roof. There was more than one person up there. A slight moan of fear passed Sarah's lips. Checking that the doors and windows were locked, she returned to the bedroom and stood by the bed, clutching the rifle tightly. She was going to protect Galley from whatever might be coming to get them. Her resolve gave her a glimmer of courage and she held onto it.

The sounds on the roof continued. She heard a rattle as someone tried the back door. Then a shattering of glass somewhere in the house as a window was smashed.

Galley continued to lie still, unaware of the danger he was in, his mind reliving its own dangerous memories.

* * *

The trouble came three days later. John had been watchful and cautious, ready to encounter the French-Canadian trappers again but they seemed to have moved on as promised. There were no more signs of their slaughter, and John felt the tense knot within him loosen. Still, he would be glad when he and Emma moved to their house in town. He realised how cut off from the other settlers they were out here in the woods. That isolation had seemed restful at first; perhaps even romantic and glamorous, but now it felt dangerous.

Also, with a baby on the way, living in town was the only option. The house was almost finished now, anyway. Perhaps a couple more weeks and the Galleys would become townies. John knew that Emma was looking forward to moving into the town's social circles. She needed people around her. Although she never complained, he saw it in her eyes sometimes when she stared out of the cabin window at the river.

He was walking by the river, knee-deep in fresh snow, when he heard her scream.

Turning and running as best he could through the snow, he knew the Delatoire brothers must have come back. He had allowed himself to be too complacent when they hadn't showed after two days, and now he was going to pay the price. He had left Emma alone in the cabin.

He had a gun, a Colt revolver, underneath his heavy coat and he seized it from where it was stuck in his belt. Loping through the snow with the gun in his hand, he felt anger and frustration rise within him. Anger at himself for leaving Emma alone. Frustration at the snow which slowed his progress.

The cabin was in sight when he heard the second scream. He saw the familiar round snowshoe tracks leading from the woods to his home. He strained with effort as he ran toward the cabin.

Then he stopped.

Pain coursed up his leg and he screamed, falling over into the deep snow as his legs failed him. The cruel steel jaws of an animal trap were locked on his right leg, just above the ankle. Lying on his side in the snow, he struggled to stay conscious. The pain made dark circles appear in his vision and he realised that if he gave in now and let that darkness wash over him, he was dead.

Alain Delatoire appeared from behind the cabin and walked toward him, grinning at John's predicament. John's gun was hidden in the snow and it was obvious from the trapper's nonchalant walk that he was unaware his trapped prey was armed. John brought the Colt up and squeezed the trigger. The French-Canadian's face exploded in a spray of red and his body collapsed to the snow, as if he was a puppet and someone had just cut his strings. He lay unmoving, a red stain spreading through the snow around his head.

John grasped the steel jaws of the trap and pulled them apart, wincing at the pain coursing up his leg from the wound where the metal had bitten into his flesh. He threw the trap away from him and staggered to his feet.

Limping painfully, he focussed on their cabin. He had to reach it.

A face appeared at the window and below that face was a rifle barrel. John whirled and the Colt exploded twice. The first bullet tore into the window frame. The second tore into the man holding the rifle. He staggered back soundlessly, the rifle falling out of the window and into the snow.

John faltered toward the door of the cabin and hesitated. He wasn't sure he wanted to see what was in there. Gathering up his courage, he kicked the door open. The man he had killed was Jean-Pierre Delatoire. He had fallen onto the crib John was building and had smashed it. He lay dead among the splinters of brightly-painted wood.

That meant Jacques was left. He had Emma. Anger and fear tore through John. As he turned from Jean-Pierre's body, a sudden movement behind startled him. He swung around in time to see the shape at the door and the Colt spoke twice, booming deafeningly in the enclosed space.

A scream was cut off by that noise. John, realising what had happened, screamed, 'No!' and ran out of the cabin, forgetting his own pain, to where the figure lay beyond the doorway.

It was Emma.

Throwing the Colt away, John ran to his dead wife and dropped to his knees next to her. Her chest and stomach were bloody but even in death she looked pretty. She looked like an angel, this woman who had come all the way from England to the New World with him because she believed in him when no one else, not even his own parents would. She had never once complained that she missed the comforts of home or that she wished she had never come to this untamed land with him. Now she was dead, as was their child within her. *He* had killed her. Tears spilled uncontrollably from him and fell onto his dead wife's pretty face.

'Hey, *monsieur*, perhaps you can't shoot too straight, eh? Perhaps you prefer killing women to men?'

John whirled and Jacques Delatoire stood before him, grinning, a rifle pointing at him. Black spots clouded John's vision again but this time, they were not brought on by pain. His pain was forgotten, buried by what made those spots whirl before him. Bloodlust. And this time, John didn't fight the blackness that appeared before him. He let it overtake him.

He leapt at the trapper, the man who had pushed Emma into his line of fire, and all thoughts of self-preservation fled. His own life meant nothing now because everything that ever mattered to him was lying dead in the snow. He heard a sound like the cry of a wild animal and he vaguely realised that it came from him. The rifle fired and he felt pain rip through his shoulder but that pain was soon buried by the bloodlust as he grabbed the trapper's throat and pulled him to the ground. The rifle spun away, out of the French-Canadian's reach.

Jacques Delatoire took a long time to die.

When it was done, Galley returned to his wife and held her lifeless body for a long time, letting grief spill from him. When that was done, he buried her, and his unborn child, by the river and returned to the cabin.

He retrieved the Colt from where he had thrown it and buried it. It was the gun that had killed his wife and he never wanted to use it again. He took the rifle from the wall of the cabin, filled a bag with food, and set fire to his home.

When the cabin was burning angrily and flames licked from the window, he turned away from it. He needed to get out of this country. He had come here expecting a new life but had found only death. He could not go home to England, back to his parents' disapproving frowns.

America. He would head south and get as far away from this pain-filled country as possible.

Perhaps even Mexico. It didn't matter. Nothing did any more.

Leaving the flaming pyre behind him, he headed into the woods.

11

Sarah's hand trembled as she gripped the rifle. After the smashing of the window, she heard the back door crash open and footsteps in the kitchen. It must be Red McCready and his men. They had known she would return and had watched the house, waiting. Not content with killing her father, they wanted to kill her as well.

Galley, unaware of the danger, continued to dream. Tears streaked down his burning cheeks. Sarah wished he would wake up. She needed him.

The doorknob twisted and Sarah let off a shot. The bullet tore a chunk of wall away. The report of the Remington in the small bedroom almost deafened her. Her ears rung crazily as the door burst open and men rushed in. Screaming and knowing that now she was going to die without ever telling

John Galley what she felt for him, she fell onto the bed, clinging to him. She prayed that he would wake up now and help her.

Strong hands tore her away and roughly stood her on her feet. She stood, shakily, facing three Indian warriors. She stifled a scream of terror. Galley had said that the Indians were savages.

A fourth Indian came through the door. He was dressed in white robes embroidered with red suns, moons and crosses. Sarah had never seen a medicine man but knew she was looking at one now. He regarded Sarah and said, 'You come with the white bear who will help my people.' He pointed to Galley.

Sarah had no idea what this man was talking about. But his eyes seemed kind as they watched her. 'Please let me go,' she pleaded. 'My friend is sick.'

The medicine man walked over to the bed and leaned over Galley, frowning. 'He is fighting fever demons.

The Great Spirit did not speak of the white bear's fever.'

A glimmer of hope reached Sarah. 'Can you help him?' she asked. 'You are a medicine man, aren't you?'

He shook his head. 'The white bear must fight with his own medicine. He fights more than just fever. I cannot help him.' He took Sarah by the arm. 'Come. The Council must be told of this.'

Sarah shook her head and fought against him but his grip was strong. 'I have to stay with him.'

He looked at her sadly. 'No one can help him. He must fight the fever. If he wins, he will live. If he loses, he will die. He must choose.' He pulled her out of the bedroom. The other Indians followed. Sarah felt despair at leaving Galley behind. She knew there was nothing more she could do to help him but she needed to be near him all the same.

'Please,' she said. 'Let me stay with him.'

The medicine man ignored her and led her outside. The Indians' horse, painted with bright red symbols, waited near the stables. The medicine man climbed onto his mount and pulled Sarah up with him. 'We will watch him,' he told her. 'You must come to our village. The Council is still undecided about the white bear. I must tell them about his fever.'

He spurred the horse on and they headed for the hills near the mountains. Sarah looked over her shoulder at the ranch house dwindling in the distance where Galley continued to fight his fever.

★   ★   ★

As they reached the village, Yellow Bird was worried. His vision had not told him that the white man would be suffering a fever. High Hawk would be sure to use this to discredit Yellow Bird's vision and persuade the Council to have the white man killed. The white woman, of course, would become part of the tribe. The other young white man, the one they had found in Blue Water Creek, would also be killed. Yellow Bird wondered if his vision *had* been wrong. He had not expected these complications.

The woman on his horse was frightened and worried about the man in the ranch house. Her body trembled against his as he rode through the village toward the Council teepee. Yellow Bird's heart went out to her.

He slipped from the horse as they reached the teepee. 'Take her to the other white man,' he told the warriors. He entered the Council teepee, trying to suppress the worry he felt for these white people. Their lives depended on whether or not he could persuade the Council to let them live.

The four clan leaders and Big Foot looked expectantly at him as he sat before them. 'Yellow Bird,' Big Foot said. 'You have found the white bear whose fate we have not yet decided?'

Yellow Bird nodded.

'Have you brought him to the village?' High Hawk asked.

'No,' Yellow Bird said. 'He is at the ranch near the mountains. He is very ill. He fights strong fever demons. I have brought his woman.'

Big Foot frowned. 'You did not tell us that the white bear would have fever,' he said.

Yellow Bird looked at his Chief. 'The Great Spirit did not tell me this.'

High Hawk looked at Big Foot. 'If Yellow Bird did not know about the fever,' he said, 'there may be other things about this white man that we do not know. He may bring this sickness to our tribe. We must kill him.'

The Chief held up a hand to silence High Hawk. 'You speak wisely, High Hawk. We cannot bring a sick man to our village. Yellow Bird was right to leave him at the white man's ranch. Before, we were undecided about this white bear. Now, the Great Spirit has taken the decision out of our hands.

The white bear is sick. We will watch him. If he dies, the Great Spirit has taken him and we must find another answer to our problem with the flame-haired one in our mountain. If the white bear lives, the Great Spirit has allowed him to live and we will bring him to our village. We will help him, as the Great Spirit told Yellow Bird we must.'

A look of anger flashed in High Hawk's eyes. 'We will let a white man dance the Ghost Dance?'

Big Foot considered for a moment then nodded slowly. 'It is in the hands of the Great Spirit now.'

* * *

The Indians took Sarah to a buffalo hide teepee and gestured for her to enter. She crouched and pushed past the hide flap which covered the entrance. Inside, sitting on a pile of furs, Todd Colton looked at her.

'What are you doing here?' Sarah

asked him. She felt angry at him for what he and his brothers had done to her and Wiley but her anger was drowned by her worry for Galley, lying ill at the ranch house. She had to get back to him.

Todd shrugged. 'The Indians caught me in the creek after Ned and Luke were killed. They brought me here, talkin' about a white bear. I had to talk to their Chief. Then, they decided I wasn't who they thought I was and I've been in this Goddamn teepee ever since.'

'They called John the white bear,' Sarah said. 'Does it mean anything to you?'

Todd shook his head. 'These Indians are crazier'n a nest full of termites. At night, I hear 'em drumming and dancing out there. Savages.'

Sarah sat down heavily on the furs. She felt tired and drained.

'Listen,' Todd said quietly. 'I'm real sorry 'bout what happened. Ned and Luke get carried away sometimes. I gotta go along with 'em because I'm their little brother. I didn't mean nothin' by it.'

Sarah said nothing. She didn't want to listen to Todd Colton repenting; she was too busy worrying about Galley and what the Indians might decide to do to him.

'Since my brothers got killed,' Todd continued, 'I've been thinking real hard about things. I'll make it up to Mr Galley and your old friend any way I can.'

'My 'old friend' is dead,' Sarah snapped. 'And John might be as well, for all I know.' She broke down, the worry and exhaustion catching up with her. She put her face in her hands and cried softly. She wished she had never come to these mountains.

Todd sat silently, looking away, embarrassed. Sarah cried until she felt even more drained than before.

Todd looked at her and said, 'I promise I'll make it up to you and Mr Galley.'

12

Galley awoke and sat up in the bed. Confused, he glanced around the room. He had never been here before. He searched his memory but everything seemed confused. He remembered a river. A cold river. And he was drifting with the current, a knife in his hand. His fever dream was still with him and at the moment seemed more real than any recent memories.

He felt hot and sticky with sweat. His face was wet with tears and he realised that he had been dreaming of Emma again. He felt sick and quickly sat up, putting his head between his knees and gagging. But his stomach was empty and he wasn't sick.

Slowly, his memory reasserted itself and he remembered Julesburg, the Colton brothers, and the killing at the bridge. How had he come to be here in this bed? The last thing he remembered was staggering through Blue Water Creek, looking for Wiley and Sarah.

Wiley and Sarah. Where were they? He listened intently. Perhaps they were in another room. But he could hear nothing. His head felt thick and heavy, his muscles weak. He knew he was ill. Swimming in the river had been a stupid thing to do.

Maybe.

At least the Coltons didn't get me on the bridge.

So?

So I saved Wiley and Sarah.

So where are they?

He got up, dressed, and gingerly walked to the door. His head pounded with every footfall. He was about to open the door when he noticed bullet holes in the wall. He ran his fingers over the punctures in the wood. Someone had fired at this door from the inside. But who? He opened the door and found himself in a hallway which led to a kitchen. Heading there, he heard his boots crunching on something and looked down. The floor was littered with broken glass. Frowning, Galley entered the kitchen. The door was open, the window smashed.

He had no idea where he was or what had happened here. Still, some sort of violence had obviously occurred. He had no gun. Before plunging into the Platte, he had packed it into his saddlebag to keep it dry.

The last time he had seen his horse was when it had bolted from the bridge. The animal was loyal and would not go far without him. Still, after he had jumped the animal onto a train and sent it to the bridge to be shot at, perhaps it had had enough and run off to a new, safer, life.

Galley stepped through the open door and into the morning sun. How long had he been in bed? He didn't carry a timepiece, so he had no idea. It was morning now, but which morning?

He looked at the surrounding landscape and remembered what Sarah had said about her father's ranch being near the mountains. This must be her ranch house. So where was she? He walked around the house and spotted the stables. Perhaps his horse was in there. But the stables were empty.

He was puzzled. The horses were gone. Sarah and Wiley were gone. What had happened?

He sat on the fence of a corral by the stables and glanced at his surroundings. The mountains looked imposing as they stretched toward the sky. Galley closed his eyes and breathed the fresh, clean air. The morning sun on his face and the warmth of the gentle breeze pleased him. He snapped his eyes open. He had no right to feel pleasure. Not while Emma lay buried in Canada.

When they had first arrived in North America, she had pointed at the logs floating downriver to the mills and said, 'You see those logs, John? The way they float aimlessly down the river is the way some people live their lives, letting life's current take them where it wants. But not us. We've got each other and we're going to go where *we* want.' At the time, he had laughed at her philosophy, but now that she was gone, he had let life drag him along with its inexorable current. And it had brought him here to the mountains.

To face Red McCready.

To die in those majestic mountains.

The thought neither pleased nor displeased him. At least the world might be a better place without him in it.

What about Sarah?

The thought of Sarah Clinton *did* please him. There was something about the woman that he found immensely attractive. She had a spirit that would not be broken. Avenging her father was a task that some women would have baulked at but she seemed to have a streak of recklessness within her. It was not the same as Galley's self-destructive recklessness. It was as if she believed that because she was doing right, some guardian angel would protect her. Her seemingly endless reserves of courage reminded Galley of Emma.

A movement in the trees to the south startled him and he leapt from the fence. A dark shape emerged from the trees slowly, coming out of the shadows and into the light. His horse.

Galley waited as the animal approached him. It shook its head at him then nuzzled him. He patted its head. 'So you found me, eh, old boy?' He inspected his mount and found burrs tangled into its mane. He checked the hooves for stones but they were clean. 'Come on,' he said to the horse. 'Let's get you watered and cleaned up.' Taking the reins, he led the animal into the stables where he found a water and feed trough. While the horse drank, Galley removed the saddle and harness and checked the saddlebags. He found his Colt and placed it in his holster.

He found horse grooming equipment in the stable and went to work on the horse. 'I'm gonna treat you better from now on,' he promised. 'No more getting shot at on bridges or jumping onto trains. OK?'

The horse shook its head as the grooming brushes tickled it. Galley continued. 'From now on, it's the good life for you. Those mountains are a bit treacherous for a horse so I'm going up on foot. I'll have more chance that way, anyway. Perhaps I can sneak up on Red and shoot him in the back, eh?' He had decided to go into the mountains alone, Sarah and Wiley's disappearance worried him but he had no way of knowing where they were. There were no tracks around the house. So he would go to the mountains to find Red McCready.

Besides, it would be better if he went to the mountains alone. He had always planned it that way. He didn't want to see anyone else dead because of him. If he failed, the only person to be killed would be him. And that would be fine.

A light thumping sound on the roof made the horse jump. Galley's gun was out almost before he realised he had drawn it.

Another thump.

Galley stood still, hardly breathing. Slight scrabbling sounds came from the stable roof. The horse was alert, ears twitching.

Someone was on the roof. Galley looked at the door and wondered if he could get out before being spotted. He doubted it. If someone was on the roof, there must be someone covering the door.

Maybe now I die.

Maybe.

He decided to rush out of the doorway, Colt ready for whatever he found on the other side. He didn't know what to expect. Maybe Red McCready and his men. Maybe another bunch of outlaws. Perhaps the Colton brother who had fled into the creek had come back with reinforcements. Whatever, Galley was ready. He would leap through the doorway, gun ready, and whatever happened, happened.

But when he finally bolted out of the stables, the sight that met his eyes shocked him. He lowered the Colt. It would be useless.

The entire ranch was crawling with Indians. They were behind him on the stable roof, positioned on the ranch house roof and lying in the dirt, waiting for him. Arrows pointed at him from every direction. Galley was amazed. He had been out here only moments ago and had no idea that anyone was close by. The Indians had taken their positions with a stealth that baffled him.

He stood still, regarding them as they watched him closely. He holstered the Colt and crossed his arms to assure them he was not going to draw. They watched him silently, arrows ready to fly.

He waited. An eerie silence descended upon the ranch. There was a tension in that silence that threatened to snap at any moment. Galley expected the arrows to come flying through that silent moment, destroying it with their whispered flight.

Nothing happened. The silence became unbearable. Finally, Galley said, 'Look, if you're going to kill me, just treat my horse well, OK? I promised him an easy life and I forgot to mention Indians. He's been through a lot lately.'

The warriors regarded him impassively. Probably couldn't understand him. But from somewhere near the ranch house came a shout in English. 'You have the medicine, white man.'

Galley squinted at the house as an Indian dressed in white robes embroidered with red wheels, suns and circled crosses came forward. He was young, and lean beneath the white robes. Galley had never seen an Indian in white robes before and wondered what tribe this man belonged to. He looked more like a ghost than a medicine man, which was what he must be attired in such robes. 'I am called Yellow Bird,' the Indian said.

'John Galley,' Galley replied. He pointed to the white and red robes. 'Are you a medicine man or what?'

Yellow Bird smiled and nodded. His gestures and bearing seemed to suggest a wisdom exceeding his age. 'I am a medicine man.' He swept his arm around. 'We are the Miniconjou, the Lakota Sioux. We come here because you have the medicine, John Galley. The Great Spirit sent me a vision that you were coming.'

Galley frowned. 'What medicine?'

The other Indians had slung their bows over their shoulders and come closer to inspect the white man. The danger seemed to be over. For now. Galley had been told that Indians had volatile natures and that the wrong word or action could set them into a killing frenzy. He would have to choose his words carefully while dealing with them. Yellow Bird said, 'You had hot plague for many days but you live. The Gods have blessed you.'

Galley shook his head. 'I'm not blessed.'

Yellow Bird looked into his eyes and an understanding crossed the medicine man's face, as if he had read something in Galley's eyes that was as clear to him as printed words. 'You were attacked by the hot plague for three days, John Galley. After we took your woman to our village, we watched you fight the hot devils. You said many things.'

Galley cursed under his breath. Wiley had said he talked in his sleep. His memories were his own. He didn't want anyone else to know what had happened in Canada. 'I must've had a bad dream,' he told the medicine man.

'No,' Yellow Bird replied, looking deeply into Galley's eyes again. 'Not dreams.'

'You said you took Sarah to your village. Why? And what about Wiley?'

Yellow Bird frowned. 'These things are for our Chief to explain. I am only medicine man. We wish you to come to our village to have many words with our wise Chief. As for your friend Wiley, he is passed into the next paradise. We watched your woman bury him in the shadows of the sacred mountains.'

Galley felt his heart sink heavily. Wiley. Dead. The old man had been Galley's only true friend. After finding him almost dead in Mexico, Wiley had helped him to a temporary recovery, getting Galley a job at Zach Jones' ranch. For a while, Galley had been lifted from his suicidal tendencies. Until Wilma Jones had died and the sight of her lying dead in the ranch house kitchen had reminded Galley of Emma lying dead in the Canadian snow, killed by his own bullets.

'I'll go see your Chief,' Galley said. He had to get Sarah back from these Sioux. 'But first I need to see Wiley's grave.'

Yellow Bird nodded and pointed behind the house. 'He lies by the mountains.'

Galley returned to the stables and retrieved an item which was buried deep in his saddlebag. Then he strode through the party of Indians to the land behind the house. No one followed him. Sarah had marked Wiley's grave with a wooden cross fashioned from two pieces of fencing. Galley stood by the marker and removed his hat, staring at the dirt under which his old friend was buried. In his hand, he held a Smith & Wesson revolver wrapped in a heavy cloth. The gun was loaded. Galley knelt and began to dig in the dirt.

The gun had been Wiley's. Many years ago, before he met Galley, Will Jones had been marshal of a small town in Arizona. But then arthritis had hit him and ended his peace-keeping career. One night, at Zach Jones' ranch, Wiley had explained to Galley that he had been a fast gunman once, and proud of it. He had given the Smith & Wesson to Galley for safe keeping until the day he was buried. 'Then I want my old iron buried with me,' he had said. Galley had promised to see that Wiley had his gun when he rested for the final time.

'I'm keeping my promise, old man,' he muttererd as he dug. He scraped out a foot-deep hole and laid the gun in it, quickly covering it with dirt again. He stood and felt a deep sense of loss. How many more would die before this was over? 'No more,' he said aloud.

Yellow Bird approached him and stood at a respectful distance. 'Are you ready to see our Chief now, John Galley?'

Galley looked at the grave of his old friend then back at the medicine man. 'Yeah,' he said. 'I'm ready.'

13

They skirted the mountains and rode into the Black Hills. Yellow Bird stayed beside Galley the whole journey, looking at the white man intently every now and again, as if he were studying an interesting piece of art. Galley felt unnerved by the attention. He had hardly ever dealt with Indians before but he had heard stories, of course.

Drunks, with too much whiskey inside them, often spouted tales of daring exploits against the Indians when they were sitting around the saloon tables. And in those stories, the Indians were always portrayed as savages. This prejudice had settled itself into Galley's mind, so that now, as he rode through the Black Hills with the Sioux, he remained alert, ready in case these savages turned on him. He was also worried about Sarah. What might they have done to her?'

Yellow Bird's scrutiny unsettled him so he decided to turn the tables. He stared at the medicine man's white robe with its red circles and crosses and said, 'I never heard of a medicine man looking like you before.'

Yellow Bird looked into his eyes and for a moment, Galley thought he had offended the Indian. But the medicine man smiled and replied, 'I wear the Ghost shirt to protect me from evil spirits and from the white man.'

'Ghost shirt?'

Yellow Bird ignored the question for a moment and turned his head on one side, as if listening for something. Then he nodded and said, 'We wear the Ghost shirts when we dance the dance of paradise; the Ghost Dance.'

Galley shook his head and frowned. He didn't want the medicine man to start spouting religion. He had heard of the Indians' mystical beliefs before. Superstitious nonsense.

But the medicine man went on. 'We

dance with the spirits of our ancestors. They are in the paradise where buffalo roam in many numbers and there is no white man. The Ghost Dance takes our spirits to them and they tell us many things.'

'Such as?' Galley asked.

'Many things,' Yellow Bird replied. 'Many things.'

'And you believe what your dead ancestors tell you?'

'Of course. Your face says you do not believe that ancestors can talk with Sioux. You are white man. You have different religion to Sioux, but you still have faith.'

Galley looked at the Indian and said flatly, 'No. I lost my faith a long time ago.'

Yellow Bird frowned. 'In our tribe, we say that a man with no faith lives only half a life. He is not whole; like a broken circle. Something very bad must have happened to you to take away religion.'

Galley looked away from the Indian

174

and stared at the sun. 'I don't want to talk about it.'

★ ★ ★

They reached the Indian village at the foot of the mountains. The teepees were brightly painted and the village swarmed with Indians going busily about their chores. As Yellow Bird's party rode toward the huddle of dwellings, shouts were heard emanating from the village and the Indians stopped what they were doing and came to see the newcomers.

Galley sat uneasily upon his saddle as he watched them flock toward him. They shouted and whooped and stared at him. Galley's hand fell automatically to the butt of his Colt. He noticed that many of the Indians wore white Ghost shirts like Yellow Bird's.

One tall, muscular warrior stepped forward and spoke in English. 'Yellow Bird, though you are wise, you bring the white man to a place where he is not welcome.'

Yellow Bird met the eyes of the warrior. 'You did not argue when I brought the white *woman* here, High Hawk. This man has fought the fever demons and won. He is the white bear of my vision. The Council has decided that we should welcome him, as we welcomed his friends. He has medicine. I bring him here to meet our wise Chief so that we may protect our sacred mountains. This man chases the flame-haired one.'

The flame-haired one? 'Red McCready?' Galley asked. 'You know where he is?'

Yellow Bird nodded and pointed toward the mountains. 'He has been seen in the mountains. He has killed some of our people. He has red hair, flame medicine. But he uses his medicine unwisely.'

'Have you tried to catch him?' Galley wondered how much chance even a man like Red McCready might have against Indians. He hoped the outlaw had managed to evade the Indians. He wanted to go up against Red himself.

'We have sent men into the mountains against him but we have not found him yet. The Great Spirit has told us that you are the man who will find him.'

'What do you think he's doing up there?'

The medicine man looked at the mountains for a moment, as if considering something, then said, 'Come, I will take you to your woman.'

They rode through the throng of Indians and dismounted near the teepees. As Galley watched his horse being led away with the others, he noticed High Hawk scowling at him. Yellow Bird tapped him on the shoulder and indicated a teepee. 'Your woman and white friend are in there.'

'White friend? My friend is dead, buried behind the ranch house.' Wondering what Yellow Bird had meant, Galley bent down and entered the teepee.

Sarah sat on a brightly coloured

woven mat in the centre of the dwelling. She was dressed in skins, like an Indian, and her beauty made Galley's breath catch in his throat. Her hair was untied and tumbled over her shoulders. When she saw Galley, she leapt up and into his arms. 'John,' she cried, 'I was so worried. You were very ill.'

He held her. She smelled wonderful; fresh with a slight scent of sweet flowers. The good feelings which swept through him as he held her depressed him. He could not replace Emma. Although his feelings for Sarah were deep, perhaps deeper than he cared to admit, he would not allow himself to indulge them. To do so would sully Emma's memory. He spotted a figure sitting quietly on the far side of the teepee.

Todd Colton looked up at him and smiled weakly. He looked at the ground as he noticed Galley watching him. Galley pushed Sarah aside and strode over to the Colton. 'What the hell are you doing here?' he demanded angrily.

178

Todd stiffened and continued to look at the ground in front of him. 'I . . . the Indians found me in Blue Water Creek. I . . . I'm sorry about what happened at the bridge.'

Galley felt anger rise hotly within him. 'My friend is dead because of you and your brothers.' He raised a fist. He needed to lash out at this young man, to release his anger over Wiley's death. Sarah grabbed his arm.

'John, no,' she said. 'It wasn't Todd's fault. His brothers are responsible for what happened at the bridge. He wanted to forget about the whole thing but they forced him to go along with it.'

'If you hadn't interfered, my friend would still be alive,' John spat angrily at the young man.

'Please, mister,' Todd pleaded, cowering away from Galley. 'I didn't mean nothing. My brothers are dead too. Please.' He collapsed to the floor and lay sobbing. 'Ned and Luke are dead. I know what we did was wrong.'

'You gave him a scare when you came

out of the river,' Sarah explained.

Galley looked at the cowering man in front of him and said, 'I should have killed him when I had the chance.' He noticed the angry look in Sarah's face and said, 'I'm sorry. I lost control. It's just that Wiley was a good friend.'

She looked at him. 'And me?'

'What about you?'

'Am I just a good friend too?'

He wanted to take her in his arms then, to crush her to him and tell her of his feelings for her. But he thought of Emma and said, 'Yes, a good friend.'

Sarah stared at him and her face flushed angrily. She started to say something but Yellow Bird entered the teepee. 'John Galley, our Chief wishes to have counsel with you.' He glanced at Sarah then left.

Galley expected Sarah to stop him leaving the teepee. She hadn't finished yet, judging by the look on her face. But she was silent as he followed Yellow Bird outside. The medicine man gestured toward the teepee and said,

'Problem with your woman?'

'No,' Galley replied, shaking his head. 'Let's go see your Chief.' He was impatient to get into the mountains to meet whatever fate awaited him there. These Sioux with their pale Ghost shirts unnerved him. Mysticism held no interest for him. If there was a God, he had dealt Galley a cruel hand and the bounty hunter wanted nothing to do with Him.

They moved to an area of the village where a group of Indian men had assembled around an elderly figure seated on the ground and wrapped in a dark blanket. 'Big Foot,' Yellow Bird said, indicating the old man. 'Our wise Chief.'

Big Foot looked at Galley. The assembled crowd did likewise. 'John Galley,' Big Foot said, his voice deep and generous, 'I invite you to join our circle. Yellow Bird told us of your coming. The Great Spirit sent him a vision in the forest. You seek the flame-haired man in the mountains.'

Galley nodded. 'I've been given the job of killing him.'

Big Foot regarded Galley closely. 'This is a dangerous job. Why do you take it? Money?'

Galley shook his head. 'I have my reasons.'

'If you kill this man, you will succeed where many Sioux have failed. I do not think you will return if you go after flame-haired man.'

'I'll take my chances,' Galley said flatly.

The Indian Chief seemed to consider for a moment, then shook his head. 'It is not wise for a white man to walk upon the sacred mountains of my people.'

'What is it with these mountains?' Galley asked, perplexed. 'Why is Red up there? Why have you sent men to kill him? What's so special about this area that you're willing to lose warriors trying to protect it?'

Big Foot stared directly at him. 'If white man knew why mountains are sacred to Sioux, he would swarm here like a dark plague. Sioux would be driven from the land. The flame-haired one learned of Sioux secret when he captured one of this tribe's women and took her to the Black Hills to use her for pleasure, then kill her. She told him secret of mountains in exchange for her life but he killed her anyway and now the flame-haired man knows Sioux secrets he has no right to know. We try to kill him, to protect our knowledge, but he is as cunning as the coyote.'

'Whatever this secret is,' Galley explained, 'I'm only interested in Red McCready — the flame-haired man. If you know where he might be up there, or why he's there, you could help me do my job. And if I kill him, I'm helping you protect your little secret.' He had no doubt that this secret would be nonsense, like everything else connected with the Indians. Like their Ghost Dance and superstitious ways.

Big Foot looked at Yellow Bird. The medicine man nodded to his Chief and

Big Foot stood and walked over to Galley. He stood in front of the bounty hunter, his dark eyes sharp and penetrating. 'Yellow Bird, who speaks wisely, says you have medicine. You survived bad fever. I think you do have medicine but do not use it wisely. You are fighting something worse than fever. You are fighting yourself. This is bad. Yellow Bird says you spoke of many things while fighting fever demons. Bad things. I think you have chance against flame-haired one because it is part of your earth-walk. But you must use strong medicine to overcome this man. You cannot fight him while you still fight yourself. We will help you. Tonight, you will dance the Ghost Dance with Sioux and tomorrow you will make peace with yourself.'

Galley snorted involuntarily. These Indians were crazy if they thought he was going to have anything to do with their twisted religion.

High Hawk stood up behind Big Foot. He was angry. 'Honoured Chief, you speak wisely, as always,' he said, trying to hold back his anger. 'But white man may not dance the Ghost Dance. It is for our people. Look how he ridicules us. He does not believe.'

Big Foot looked from Galley to High Hawk. 'We spoke of this after Yellow Bird told us of his vision. The Council, of which you are part, agreed to let the white bear dance the Ghost Dance. He will see things differently after he communes with his spirits.'

Galley looked at High Hawk. He had taken an immediate dislike to the Indian the moment he had met him. If he joined in their dance, it would make the warrior even angrier. Good. He looked at Big Foot and said, 'All right, let's dance.'

14

Drums were brought out from the teepees and arranged around a small hill near the mountains. Big Foot led his people and Galley to the foot of the hill. The atmosphere was electric. Galley tried to remain calm but a tangible wave of excitement swept through the Indians and caught him in its swell. He felt a shiver of anticipation run down his spine, even though he knew this dance was just a crazy Indian superstition.

Someone threw a white Ghost shirt at him and he looked at its brightly painted designs, frowning.

'Wear it,' Big Foot said.

Galley shrugged, slipped it over his head and felt foolish. The shirt reached down to his knees, like a nightgown. But unlike a nightgown, it was garish with its painted suns, moons, stars and circles.

Indians began to pound on the drums. The beat sounded like a thunderous heartbeat, so loud that the entire prairie seemed to vibrate with it. Ghost shirt-clad dancers started to gyrate with the sound, dancing around the perimeter of the hill. Yellow Bird appeared at Galley's shoulder. 'Now is the time to dance, John Galley,' he said.

'What do I do?' Galley asked.

The medicine man smiled. 'Just dance.' He pointed to Galley's temple. 'You have much going on in here. Forget it. Do not listen to the voices inside your head; listen only to the drums. Do not let your actions be controlled by thoughts; simply dance. Let your spirit ride the drumbeat.' He pointed to the hill, which was now swarming with dancers spinning and jerking with the drumbeat. 'Go now and dance.'

Galley walked toward the hill, feeling the beat vibrating through the ground beneath his feet and up his legs into his body. He wasn't much of a dancer. He and Emma used to attend a barn dance once a month in Canada but he was cursed with two left feet. He would sometimes have the place in an uproar as he exaggerated his clumsy movements around the dance floor, playing up to the crowd and to his wife with joyful abandon.

Happier times.

He looked at the Indians around him on the hill and realised there was no set movement to the Ghost Dance. Some jerked to a rhythm of their own while others spun and twisted their bodies gracefully in time with the heavy drumbeat. All eyes were closed.

Joining the flow of bodies, Galley closed his own eyes and started moving. At first he flailed about clumsily, trying to get the beat. Then he relaxed into the monotonous pounding and let his body do whatever it wanted to do. The drumbeat seemed to grow louder, as if it had synchronised with his own heartbeat and controlled the flow of his blood as he danced around the hill.

Soon, it seemed as if the entire prairie danced with that beat. The earth seemed to swell beneath his feet and for a moment, Galley wondered if he had finally gone crazy. Perhaps the Indians, already knowing about his fragile mind, had decided that the dance would break it for good. One more crazy white man out of the way. But then it didn't matter. All that mattered was the drumbeat. Monotonous. Monotonous. Monotonous.

He danced and swirled and twisted with the droning beat.

Time lost all meaning. He had no idea if he had been dancing for minutes or hours. His mind seemed to be dancing into twisted convolutions the same as his body. He was aware of nothing but the beat, the ceaseless beat. The beat of the drums; the beat of the prairie; the beat of his heart.

Then, suddenly, he was aware of something else. He was falling, totally exhausted, to the ground.

When he opened his eyes, he was in the cabin in Canada.

He jerked upright, his head still pounding with the beat. But the beat was gone now, to be replaced by the silence of the Canadian winter. The wind whispered through the eaves of the cabin but that was all. He looked around in panic. 'This isn't possible,' he told himself.

But it was true. He was in the cabin. He could feel the cold winter air on his skin and smell the forest outside.

The cabin was exactly as he remembered it. His rifle hung on the wall. Emma's needlework sat piled in one corner. The crib sat, unfinished, near the wall.

'I burned this place to the ground,' Galley whispered.

He stood up and felt dizzy. He sat down at the small table and massaged his temples. How could he be here? A more powerful thought struck him and he sat up, his heart racing. If the cabin was still standing, was Emma here?

No, of course not. Emma was dead. He had killed her himself.

But he had also burned down the cabin and now, here he was sitting inside it.

He looked toward the door. If he went out, would he find Emma's body sprawled in the snow? No, he couldn't bear to see that sight again.

Yet part of him had to know.

Slowly, painfully, he walked to the door and placed a hand on the rough wooden handle. Taking a deep breath of cold winter air, he pushed the door open and walked outside.

His wife lay dead in the snow.

She was just as he remembered, lying in the snow as if asleep, a vision of beauty corrupted by a bullet. *His* bullet. Galley knelt down in the cold snow and looked at her peaceful face. How everything would have been different if only he hadn't killed her! He felt tears well in his eyes. 'Oh, God,

Emma, I'm so sorry,' he whispered.

'Sorry for what, John?' The voice came from behind him. Emma's voice. He whirled round and she stood by the cabin, smiling at him. He looked back at her dead body in the snow. Confused, he stood up and went to her.

He took her in his arms and squeezed her tightly. 'Oh God, Emma, I thought I'd lost you.' He felt the tears in his eyes spill over and run down his cheeks, onto his wife's shoulder. He stroked her hair. It was his Emma. He could feel her, smell her, kiss her.

She looked at him and smiled. But there was a sadness in her eyes. 'John,' she said softly.

'I thought I'd lost you,' he continued. 'I've missed you so much.'

She pushed him gently away from her. 'John,' she said, more firmly now. 'Look there in the snow.' He looked and there was her dead body, still looking as if she were just resting. He turned back to the Emma in his arms.

'You have lost me,' she said.

He felt confused, lost. 'What's happening?'

'This is your vision, John. You aren't really here; you're in the Sioux village. The Ghost Dance brings visions to the Indians. This is *your* vision.'

Emma looked pityingly at him. 'I'm here to stop that, John.'

He shook his head again. 'You can't stop it, I need to see this, to remember what I did to you.'

She laid her hands gently on his chest. 'No,' she said. 'You need to forget this. We had so many good times together, John. Is this all you can remember of me? A body in the snow?'

'I killed you,' he whispered softly.

She smiled gently. 'No, John. The Delatoire brothers killed me. I was pushed into your line of fire.'

'I know that but I pulled the trigger.'

She wiped the tears from his cheeks. 'You're guilty of something much worse than that, John.'

He looked into her eyes. 'What do you mean?'

'Every day since then, you've been trying to kill yourself. The man I married wasn't a bounty hunter. He hated violence. He was gentle. Look what's hapened to you. You've let the violence of that day infect you. Let it go. Live your life. Don't throw it away. I don't want you to throw it away.'

'I deserve to die for what I did to you.'

'Your problem,' she said, 'is that all you remember is this ugly scene. Remember the good times, John. The bad time is over. Let it be over. Stop torturing yourself. It wasn't your fault.'

'Of course it was my fault!' He pushed away from her and stumbled back to the cabin. He did not want to look at the body any longer. He had seen it too many times in his night-mares. He sat down inside the cabin. Emma came in after him and stood in front of him, hands on her hips.

'Now you listen to me,' she said angrily. 'No one can change what happened that day. Jacques Delatoire

194

pushed me into your line of fire. I don't blame you. Nobody blames you but yourself. You're punishing yourself for no reason. You're throwing your life away.'

'I miss you,' he said pathetically.

'Of course you do. But you're still alive.' She took his hand in both of hers. 'Live life, John. Don't throw it away.'

He knew deep down that what Emma said was true. He was still alive and that was precious. He felt his sorrow lifting, like a heavy weight being taken from his shoulders. 'I know you're right, Emma,' he said. 'But I don't want to forget you.'

'You won't forget me,' Emma said. 'But forget this one sad day out of the many good ones we had together.' She moved to him and put her arms around him. He moved his face toward hers to kiss her.

★ ★ ★

And woke up on the hill, the beat of the drums still strong and vibrant. He sat up quickly and his head swam. Around him, some Indians still danced wearily while most lay on the ground. It looked as if someone had killed half of the tribe. They lay unmoving and Galley knew that they were hallucinating as he had been. Staggering to his feet, he fought a wave of nausea and stumbled down the hill.

Yellow Bird came over to him. The medicine man looked solemn. 'You have seen the power of the Ghost Dance, John Galley.'

Galley felt disoriented. His experience during the dance had shocked him. He had not expected anything to happen. The vision frightened him. 'I don't know,' he said. 'I had a dream, a vivid dream. I feel . . . dislocated and confused. As if I left some part of myself in the dream.'

The medicine man nodded as if he understood completely. 'You need rest. When the sun touches you tomorrow, you will see clearly. I can see it in your eyes already. The pain is going. Come.' He led Galley back through the village toward the teepee.

Galley noticed that the sky was darkening rapidly. 'How long have I been on the hill?'

Yellow Bird regarded him closely. 'Long enough.' They reached the teepee. 'Now you must rest. You have communed with your spirits and tonight you will sleep well.' He turned and walked back toward the hill where the Ghost Dance continued.

Galley entered the teepee and lay down heavily on the pile of furs. Despite the fact that he had been dreaming on the hill, he was exhausted. His mind felt numb and he needed sleep. He realised with a start that someone else was in the teepee, sitting in the shadows across from him. 'Sarah,' he said.

Her voice sounded tremulous as she spoke. 'John, I don't want you to go after Red McCready any more.'

'But he killed your father,' he said flatly. He still felt numb and was in no mood for an argument with Sarah.

'I don't care any more,' she replied. 'I can see that some things Wiley told me in Julesburg are true. I don't know what happened to you in the past but one thing is obvious: you want to die.' She started to cry softly. 'Well I don't want you to die because of me. Forget Red McCready. Go on working as a bounty hunter if you want and maybe some day you'll get your wish and someone will be quicker than you with a gun. You'll end up buried in an unmarked grave in some forgotten town God-knows-where. But I don't want to see you kill yourself.'

She began to sob and Galley lay there in the dark, listening to her. He realised that these were the same words Emma had said to him in his dream. Sarah seemed distant as he lay there. His mind was calm, almost blank. Perhaps another time he might have gone to her and put his arms around

198

her, comforting her. Perhaps they would embrace and fall together to the furs.

But not now. Galley could feel no emotion. He felt as if all feelings had been drained out of him by the Ghost Dance and his subsequent vision of Emma.

So Sarah cried in the darkness and he lay unmoving and unmoved on the furs. Eventually, he felt sleep creep over him and he let it take him. He awoke momentarily as Sarah left the teepee and he saw her illuminated by the moonlight; he wondered dimly why she had dressed in her shirt and pants and why she was carrying a gun.

Then sleep overtook him again and he slept.

15

The following morning, Galley woke up fast. His tiredness had disappeared during the night and he felt fully rested and energised. He climbed off the pile of furs and out of the teepee.

The morning was dull, with dark angry clouds hanging low in the sky but the weather did nothing to temper Galley's mood. He felt elated. Looking up at the mountains, he noticed their beauty for the first time. Watching the Indians around him, going about their daily chores, he felt a kinship which he had never felt before. These people had danced on the hill with him, had shared his visions.

Was the Ghost Dance responsible for his new outlook? Surely not. A dream could not affect him so strongly. He had dreamed of Emma before and he had never woken up feeling so elated.

Those dark dreams usually put him in a black mood the following day. But not this time.

Was there something to the dance after all? No, he reasoned. A white man could not find penance for his soul in an Indian mystical dance. Still, he couldn't argue with the fact that he felt somehow lighter, as if a great weight had been lifted from his shoulders. And there was something else as well, some deeper change which he couldn't yet understand.

'John Galley.' Yellow Bird approached him, smiling. He looked at Galley and nodded. 'You have communed with your spirits.'

Galley frowned. 'I don't know about that. I slept well last night and I feel good today.'

The medicine man grinned widely. 'What you believe does not matter so much as what you become. Yesterday, you were a man who fought with the worst enemy: himself. Now, you have called a truce. Whether you believe this is because you slept well or whether you believe the Ghost Dance allowed you to talk to your guiding spirits does not matter. The result is the same.'

Galley considered for a moment then shrugged. 'Maybe.' Then he realised what had changed deep within him. 'Last night Sarah said it was obvious I wanted to die. Maybe she was right. But not any more. Now, I don't want to die any more. I've been missing out on a lot of things because of my feelings. They're gone now and I want to live life as I was meant to.'

The mention of Sarah brought last night's conversation back to him and he felt a sudden need to find her. He would tell her what he felt for her. He could do that now, without remorse. He had not stopped loving the memory of Emma, but he now understood that he must live his life and come to terms with his past. And he wanted to share the rest of his life with Sarah.

'Last night,' he told the medicine man, 'she told me to forget going after

Red McCready and that suits me just fine. I don't think I could get the drop on him and I don't want to get killed any more.' He looked up at the towering mountains. 'So I guess your secret is going to have to be protected by your own people. I won't be going into the mountains to get McCready.' He thought for a moment, then added, 'I don't know where I go from here, but I'm putting my shooting days behind me.'

Yellow Bird clapped him on the shoulder. 'And you think this change is because of a good sleep?' He laughed. 'Come, John Galley, we will find your woman. She will be pleased with your new face. You smile where you used to frown.'

They halted as Todd Colton came running up to them, shouting. 'Galley,' the young man called. 'Galley. Have you seen Sarah?' He skidded to a halt in front of the two men.

'No,' Galley replied, suddenly sensing trouble. 'Why?'

'She was talkin' mighty strange yesterday after you went off with the medicine man. It sounded like she was thinking of goin' after Red McCready herself. I thought she was just blowin' smoke at the time, but I can't find her anywhere this mornin'.'

The glimpse of Sarah in the moonlight last night came back to Galley. 'Damn, I saw her last night with her rifle. She's gone into the mountains on her own.' He felt fear like a tight iron band around his chest. Why hadn't he spoken to her last night? Why hadn't he told her how he felt? He cursed himself and looked at the imposing mountains. A woman alone up there didn't stand a chance against a hardcase like Red McCready.

He turned to Yellow Bird and said, 'Looks like I'll be going after Red after all.' He felt the band of fear tighten. He didn't want to go into these mountains. He wanted to live more than he had wanted anything since Emma's death. And now, he had to risk his life just as he was beginning to appreciate how precious it was.

'I'll come with you,' Todd Colton offered. 'I figure I owe you something.'

'No,' Galley said.

'I can shoot good,' Todd continued. 'I want to help you.'

'No,' Galley repeated.

'We'll have more chance if there's two of us.'

'I said no. I don't want your death on my hands. Look, why don't you ride back to Julesburg? No hard feelings.' He held out his hand. Todd hesitated and looked as if he was going to argue, then shook Galley's hand.

'No hard feelings,' Todd said. He turned and walked away.

Galley turned to Yellow Bird. 'You going to tell me what Red's after up there? It might help me to find him.'

The medicine man frowned and shook his head. 'My Chief says I cannot tell white man secret of mountains. Flame-haired one knows secret but not where to find it. He could be anywhere, searching. If you kill him, you will do us a great service.'

'I'll try,' Galley replied. He looked at his hands. They had saved his life on numerous occasions, automatically drawing and firing his gun at the right time, with deadly accuracy. But that automatic reflex had come when Galley had wanted to die and did not worry about his survival. Now that he wanted to live, would that reflex desert him? Would his mind be so preoccupied worrying about the outcome of an encounter that his brain would fail to recognise the optimum moment to draw and shoot?

As a test, Galley pulled the Colt from his holster and held it in front of him. It felt awkward and clumsy. If this was how he was going to draw when facing Red McCready, he had no chance.

Thunder rumbled and the first drops of rain fell from the sky.

16

The rain was coming down heavily as Galley climbed the mountain, following a fast-flowing stream. He had lost his waterproof poncho in the North Platte River but the Indians had given him a jacket made of hide, which kept him warm and dry. He proceeded cautiously along the stream, alert for any sound other than the hissing of the rain, for any movement other than the small animals and birds which darted among the pines. The weather made it impossible for him to try and track Sarah.

He vowed to himself that this was the last time he went after anyone carrying a gun. It was a pattern of destruction that he had played out many times in his life, starting with the Delatoire brothers and ending now with Red McCready. In fact, if he found Sarah before he found McCready, he would take her down the mountain and avoid an encounter with McCready altogether.

He wondered if Tom Riley and Bill Jakes were up there with McCready. If so, that was even more reason to avoid a confrontation.

His worry for Sarah felt like a tight knot in his gut. He tried to forget his emotions; they would just get in the way if it came to a shootout with McCready. He was a man, though, and worrying about a woman he cared for was part of his makeup. He pushed on up the mountain, desperate to find Sarah.

★　★　★

Sarah huddled beneath an outcropping of rock. Not because she was sheltering from the rain, but because she heard voices. She couldn't locate the direction they were coming from so she had hidden here. It would do no good to go blundering into Red McCready's camp unprepared. She held the Remington tightly as she huddled there, shivering. She was soaked to the skin. She wondered if it had been wise to come up here alone.

Better that than see John Galley get killed. She couldn't bear that. If Red and his men killed her, no one would care.

Galley didn't care.

She supposed she was a fool to have fallen for a bounty hunter. And for one with a death wish, in particular. She had tried to make him see how much she cared for him, tried to tell him. But he had withdrawn to that secret place in his mind where he relived some dark memory.

Perhaps she was better off without him. Perhaps she was better off dead. At least she was going to try to avenge her father's death. She listened intently. The voices continued, to her right.

She crawled out from under the rocks and crouched, listening. The voices were coming from the trees ahead. Carefully, she crawled through the wet carpet of pine needles to the trunk of a tree and cautiously peered around it.

There was no one there. But the voices were coming from that direction. Flattening herself against the rocks, Sarah crept further into the trees, the scent of damp pine strong in her nose. The voices were louder now, but she still could not see anyone.

'I'm tellin' ya, we should pack up and move out. It ain't here,' the first voice said.

The reply came from Red McCready. Sarah recognised the voice from the time he had visited her father's ranch. 'It's here, Tom. That Clinton fella knew it. Why do ya think he built his goddamn ranch so close to the mountains? And that Indian girl knew it, too. Them Indians think this mountain's holy or somethin'.'

'We been here a month and we ain't found nothin', Red.'

'Well I thought that Clinton would tell me where it was but he made out he didn't know anythin' about it, so I had to kill him. So now we got to find it ourselves.'

At the mention of her father, Sarah felt rage boil up inside her. She might as well go for McCready now. It was as good a time as any. She strode forward through the trees, the Remington ready.

The sound of a gun being cocked behind made her spin round. A huge, bearded man stood before her. He held a revolver pointed at her. 'Now what's a pretty thing like you doin' with a gun, sweetheart?'

She hesitated. If she shot at this man now, she would destroy any chance she had of surprising McCready. Still, if she didn't shoot him, he would probably shoot her before she could get to McCready anyway.

'Drop that rifle,' he said. Then he shouted, 'Red, Tom, we got us a visitor.'

Sarah looked over her shoulder and saw Red McCready and a thin blond man emerge from the rocks. She realised that the reason she hadn't seen them earlier was because they were in a cave. Red saw her and grinned evilly. 'Well, if it isn't Miss Clinton. Allow me to introduce my friends. This here's Tom Riley and the fella with the gun on ya is Bill Jakes.' He looked at Riley. 'Perhaps Miss Clinton will be willing to tell us things her daddy wouldn't.'

Sarah considered turning around and shooting McCready. She still held the rifle. But she doubted if she would be able to aim it before Jakes shot her.

'Why don't you put that rifle down and come in out of the rain,' McCready said. 'We got things to discuss.'

'I don't know anyhing about why the Indians think this mountain's sacred,' Sarah said.

'Well now, that's what your daddy said just before I shot him,' McCready said, grinning.

Sarah spun around then, bringing the rifle up, not caring any more if she was killed or not. A shot at McCready would be worth it. As she turned, she felt pain explode along her neck and shoulders and she collapsed to the ground, managing to squeeze off a shot but missing Red McCready. She heard the bullet ricochet harmlessly off the rocks before blackness overcame her.

* * *

Galley dove for cover at the sound of the shot. His Colt was out before he realised the noise had come from too far away for the shot to have been aimed at him. He slipped the Colt back into its holster, leaning against the trunk of a tree and breathing hard. The climb was arduous and the muddy ground made it more so.

What that shot meant, Galley could only wonder. If McCready had killed Sarah . . . he pushed the thought from his mind.

He guessed at the direction the shot had come from and started to move through the trees toward the source of the sound. He was even more alert now, and he felt an emotion he had never associated with hunting men before: fear. Until now, he had never cared if he lived or died and hunting and killing men had prompted no emotion at all. But now, he could taste his fear like burning copper in his mouth.

He left the trees behind and entered a gully where the stream babbled noisily through the rocks. He needed a rest after the long climb. He sat on the rocks and watched the swelling stream as it wound its way down the mountain.

Something in the water caught his attention and he stared at the spot where he had seen it. But it was gone. He looked again and there it was; a flash in the water. Kneeling, he put his hand into the cold water and scooped up a handful of dirt from the bottom. Allowing the water and mud to sift through his fingers, he examined it closely.

He knew why Red McCready was so interested in this mountain. He knew why the Indians regarded the place as holy and didn't want the white man to come here.

He saw it glinting in his palm.

He glanced further upstream.

He looked at the tiny sparkling grains in his hand.

He had found the mountain's secret. Gold.

★ ★ ★

He moved through the gully quickly, seeking the shelter of the trees again. He knew why Red McCready was up here; he knew about the gold. He must have reasoned that Sarah's father, living so close to the mountains, had known about it as well and brought him up here to try to force Clinton to tell him where the precious metal was hidden.

Galley didn't care about the gold. He wanted Sarah back, unharmed. He knew that the Indians were right to want to keep the gold a secret. If word got round that gold had been found here, a gold rush would occur. Shanty towns would spring up all over the area and the Indians would be driven from the land. They were right to fear the white man finding out about their sacred mountain.

'Hold it right there, mister.' The voice came from behind him. Galley felt a knot of fear tighten in his stomach as he turned around. Two men stood before him, guns trained on him. Tom Riley and Bill Jakes. Galley realised that he had no chance against two men. Their guns were out, his holstered. And worse than that, he was afraid. His hand was trembling.

Maybe now I die.

That thought made the knot of fear in his stomach tighten even more. He had so much to live for now. He couldn't die, not before he had told Sarah that he loved her.

'You think we should take him to Red?' Jakes asked his companion.

Riley shook his head. 'Nah, let's kill 'im.'

They cocked their guns and Galley's mind raced. This was the moment when his thoughts usually stopped and his body took over, doing the killing for him. But now, his mind spun crazily. He couldn't shoot both of them. Maybe one. Which one? Could he draw in time? When should he draw? He froze and realised that it was too late; the time to draw his gun had come and gone and he had missed it. A shot rang out.

Bill Jakes fired his gun but the shot went wild, into the trees. Because Jakes was being spun through the air like a demented ballet dancer, blood spurting from his neck, spraying the rocks as he fell.

Riley didn't shoot at all because he saw what had happened to his companion. A look of surprise crossed his face and that split second meant the time for Galley to draw had returned. He pulled the Colt from his holster and let off a shot.

He missed.

Either the gun grip was too wet or his hand was trembling too much, but the shot went wide and Riley, regaining his composure, returned his attention to Galley.

Another shot rang out and blood erupted from Riley's chest. But as he went down, the blond man fired and Galley felt pain rip through his right thigh. He dropped his Colt and it splashed into the stream. Galley fell to the rocks, holding his bleeding thigh.

Todd Colton appeared from the trees, whooping and holding a rifle above his head. 'You see that, Galley? Bill Jakes and Tom Riley and I got 'em both. Maybe I should take up bounty hunting like you. Maybe I . . . ' He stopped as a shot cracked from the trees. Todd went sprawling headlong into the stream, the look of joy on his face transformed into one of surprise. He landed face down in the water and didn't get up again.

Galley knew Red McCready was in the trees. He wondered desperately if he would have time to pick up Riley's or Jakes' gun before the next shot came. He didn't dare, so he turned and half-ran, half-limped for the cover of the trees. Pain lanced up his leg and blood ran down his thigh, leaving a clear trail for McCready to follow. It would only be a matter of time now.

17

Thunder rumbled and the sky was growing dark as Galley fled through the trees. He glanced behind him occasionally but could see no sign of his pursuer. McCready was staying back, waiting for his moment to strike. Or perhaps he had elected not to chase Galley from behind and was now circling through the trees either to the left or to the right, ready to ambush his quarry. Galley knew that McCready was sly.

He stumbled over the wet, slippery ground, his mind racing. What could he do to escape? Wounded and bleeding, he had no chance against McCready. Even before, his chances against such a vicious outlaw were slim; now, they were nonexistent.

He only wished he could know if Sarah were still alive. Had Red captured her or was she still searching the mountain for him? Galley feared the first but prayed for the second. He wondered if Sarah was dead somewhere, another victim of this manhunt.

Too many people had died already. Wiley, Ned and Luke Colton, Todd Colton. Bill Jakes and Tom Riley. Death sickened Galley. Since Emma's death, he had surrounded himself with killing. He had waded through rivers of blood. No more.

He noticed an outcropping of rock and considered hiding beneath it. No, he was sure to be found and he had no gun. He had to run. It was his only hope.

He followed the wet rocky wall through the trees as the rain began to come down heavier and angrier. It hissed as it blanketed the rocks and trees and Galley knew that if McCready were right behind him, he would never hear his pursuer over the noise of the downpour. But that also worked to his advantage; McCready wouldn't be able to hear him either. He tried to ignore the shooting pain in his leg and realised how lucky he was to be alive.

Todd Colton had obviously followed him into the mountains. The boy was stubborn. He had seemed to be trying to right the wrongs of the past. Galley knew all about that. As it turned out, Todd's refusal to listen to him in the Indian village had saved Galley's life. And ended Todd's.

His own shooting performance at the stream worried him. His gunfighter's instincts had left him along with his nonchalant attitude toward death. He could no longer shoot. When he wanted to die, he shot well. Now he wanted to live, he couldn't protect himself. The irony made him grin, despite the pain from his leg.

He stumbled along the rocks until he saw something ahead which might offer a place to hide. A cave.

He squinted against the rain, looking for McCready. If the outlaw saw him slip into the cave, he would be trapped.

But he couldn't see the redheaded outlaw anywhere.

He slipped inside, into the blackness. A shuffling sound in the darkness made him think he had walked into a trap. McCready was in here, already waiting for him and in a moment he would hear a shot and feel the bullet ripping into him.

But he heard a whimper and realised it was a woman. 'Sarah?' he whispered.

'John?' Her voice sounded frightened, then, when she knew it was him, stronger. 'You followed me.'

'Thank God I found you,' he said, searching for her in the dark. Despite his painful wound, he felt joy pushing through him. Sarah was alive!

'Bill Jakes pistol-whipped me,' she said. 'They tied me up in here and went out looking to see if anyone had come with me. They didn't believe a woman would come up here alone.'

'Well, you shouldn't have,' Galley said. He tried to sound stern but the fact that Sarah was alive made his voice tremble with happiness.

'I was mad at you,' Sarah said. 'I got some ideas into my head about . . . me and you. When I could see that they were crazy ideas and there was no chance . . . for us, I came to get Red myself. I'm sorry.'

'Those ideas weren't crazy,' Galley told her. 'I'm here aren't I? I'm the one who had crazy ideas. I think I'm over them now.' He thought for a moment, then took her into his arms. 'I know I am.'

He kissed her. 'McCready's following me,' he said. 'He's killed Todd Colton.'

A small, frightened sound escaped from her lips.

'I don't have my gun,' Galley explained. He held her tightly in the darkness. It felt good to hold her.

'You can't stay here, he'll find you,' Sarah said. 'This cave isn't far from the ranch house. The horses are still in the stables there. You can go and get help. Maybe the Indians . . . '

'The ranch house?' An idea crossed his mind.

'Yes, take a horse and get out of here.'

'I'm not leaving you. How do I get to the house?'

'There's a stream to the south. It runs onto the ranch. Get a horse and . . . '

'No,' he said, 'I'll be back.' He let go of her and rushed to the cave mouth.

'John,' she said. 'I . . . '

'I'll be back,' he repeated and stumbled out into the rain.

He limped along the slippery rocks, wondering how close McCready was. He couldn't think about that now. He had to get to the ranch house. He found the stream and started to follow it down the mountainside as night closed in all around him. He heard noises in the trees and wondered which ones were nocturnal animals and which ones might be Red McCready, hunting for him.

Red's voice called from the trees to

his left, startling him. It sounded close. Too close. 'There's no point runnin',' McCready called. 'I'm gonna find ya.'

Galley stopped and tried to gauge the exact location of the voice but the rain and the echo off the rocks made it impossible. He splashed into the stream in an attempt to wash the blood off his leg and hide his bloody trail. He slipped on the rocks and fell into the cold water.

'You goin' swimmin', boy?' the voice was closer now.

Galley struggled to his feet, cursing his own clumsiness, and continued along the stream. Lightning arced in the sky and Galley saw what might have been the ranch house in the distance. He quickened his pace as much as his bleeding leg would let him.

'When I've finished with you, me and the pretty lady are goin' to have us a mighty fine time,' McCready taunted and Galley was startled by how close the voice sounded now. He splashed out of the stream as lightning flashed again. Yes, the ranch house was up ahead. He veered toward it.

* * *

Red McCready was having fun. Whoever this feller was, he was providing some mighty fine sport. This was like hunting a wounded rabbit. The feller was unarmed and that fact didn't bother Red at all. It made it more fun. When he finally caught up with his prey, he could take his time shooting him. He'd be able to watch the man's eyes as he realised he was going to die.

Throughout his career as a thief and murderer, Red had enjoyed watching people die. At the moment of death, they got a look in their eyes, a kind of surprised look, that he liked to see.

Red liked that look and the knowledge that he — Red McCready — had put it there.

He heard splashing again further downstream and tried to peer through the darkness. He knew he was close now — the splash had been loud — and he knew that his prey was slowing. But the night was too black for him to see anything. Lightning flashed and he did see something: his quarry, limping toward the Clintons' ranch house. Red smiled to himself and followed.

The fact that Tom Riley and Bill Jakes were dead didn't bother Red at all. It just meant there would be more gold for him when he finally found it. Perhaps the Clinton girl would talk. Or maybe she would be like her father; he had insisted that he knew nothing of any gold. Red didn't believe that; the man had built his ranch so close to the mountains he *must* have known something. But he had taken the secret to his grave. If his daughter talked, fine; if not, Red still intended to have some fun with her before he finally killed her. Hell, he was going to have a lot of fun with her whether she talked or not.

He giggled to himself as lightning arced across the sky, illuminating the ranch house with a ghostly light. The feller was limping across the land behind the house but he wasn't going toward the building. He had turned to his left and was skirting along the rocks at the base of the mountain.

Red had thought the feller would head for the house, maybe hole up in there, but obviously the man was trying to trick him by doing the unexpected. Fine. Red would play his game. He had a gun and he wasn't wounded. The odds were stacked in his favour.

As the lightning passed, the night's blackness hid the feller from Red's sight. Red followed the stream down to the rocks near where he had last seen his prey. When the lightning flashed again, Red would have him.

He wondered if the feller was going to try and hide in the rocks. If that was the case, Red would have fun flushing him out. But then he saw a shape in the darkness, standing still by the rocks.

It was the feller. Probably exhausted. Or dying from the wound in his leg. Or maybe he just realised he couldn't run forever. 'I see ya, feller,' Red shouted, running up to the figure.

He stopped twenty yards in front of the figure. It was too dark. He couldn't see the feller's eyes. He wanted to see that death-look as he killed him. He would have to wait for the next flash of lightning to see the fear etched on the man's face. 'I got ya now,' he said into the blackness.

'I guess you do,' came the reply. The voice was calm, even. That made Red mad. He decided that when the lightning came again, he would shoot the feller in his good leg. See how calm he felt then.

'You didn't run too fast, now did ya?' he said.

'I'm through running,' the man said. Flat, unpanicked.

Red was growing angrier. He wanted the man to be scared, pleading for his life. Where was that goddamn lightning? He held his gun loosely at his side. He was in no danger; the feller was unarmed and wounded. And when the lightning came again, he would be even more wounded. Then again at the next flash, then again at the one after that. Red would make him scared. He would blow him to pieces slowly. He giggled to himself as lightning flashed, casting an eerie glow over everything.

Red stopped giggling and arced his gun upwards. And as he did so, he took in the scene before him.

The feller was standing just where Red thought he was but there was something else as well. Something next to him. A wooden cross, illuminated in the stark ghostly light. Its long shadow fell over the feller's face, hiding it. A grave marker. And Red could see that there was a hole dug in the wet earth near the marker. And a piece of cloth was blowing about in the wind.

And the feller had a gun!

The realisation came too late to Red. As soon as he saw the revolver in the man's hand, he froze in surprise. And as he froze like a scared animal, he knew that the look he enjoyed seeing in other men's eyes as they realised they were going to die was now in his own eyes.

The man's gun spat twice and Red felt hot pain explode in his chest.

As he fell to the wet earth, lightning flashed again and Red saw the man standing by the gravemarker, watching him die, the gun in his hand smoking. Red managed to turn his face away; no one was going to see fear in Red McCready's eyes. And fear was what he knew was there. He closed them as the pain in his chest spread through his whole body; burning, as if his entire body was being engulfed with hot flame.

Then he died.

★ ★ ★

Galley picked up the cloth from the ground and wrapped Wiley's Smith & Wesson back into it. He knelt down over his old friend's grave and buried the gun back in the soft earth. He stood over the grave for a moment before heading back up the mountain.

'It's over, Wiley,' he said. 'The killing is over.'

He looked up at the dark mountain. Sarah was up there, waiting for him.

'I've got a life to go to now, Wiley,' he said. 'The past is over and done with.'

He had some things to do before he went back to the cave to get Sarah. It was going to be a long night.

The rain stopped as he headed up the dark mountain.

18

The rain stopped but the sky still looked dark and angry as Galley climbed back up the mountain. He swore an oath to himself that Red McCready would be the last person he ever killed. He had had enough killing to last a lifetime.

Things were going to be different now. He had Sarah to think about. As he scrambled up the muddy mountainside, he ached to see her. But he had other things to attend to first.

He headed toward the stream where Todd Colton had saved his life.

★　★　★

By the time he reached the cave, the thunderheads had passed over and had been replaced by less-threatening grey clouds. The pine trees smelled strong in the wet, fresh air. Galley slipped into the cave. 'Sarah?'

'John?' She sounded worried. 'Are you all right? You've been gone ages.'

He groped for her in the dark and found her. He held her to him. She was cold. 'Red McCready is dead,' he said.

She let out a sigh of relief. Her father had been avenged, finally. 'Are you hurt?' she asked Galley.

He shook his head, realised that she couldn't see him in the dark and said, 'No, I'm fine.' He kissed her cold forehead. 'Better than ever. Come on, we'd best get back to the Sioux village and get warm. They'll be worrying about us. Big Foot will be glad to know we've solved their problem for them.'

He untied her and she followed him out of the cave, rubbing her limbs where the ropes had been. She stumbled and he caught her. She looked at him closely. 'Are you really OK, John?'

He nodded. 'Maybe it *was* the Ghost Dance or maybe I've just changed but I see everything differently now. No more death wish. I want to live more than ever. I have a lot to thank Yellow Bird for.'

'I'm just sorry for Wiley,' Sarah said. 'He didn't deserve to die in the circumstances he did. I liked him a lot.'

'Yeah,' Galley replied. 'I think he would have rather died out on the trail than quietly in his bed, though. Wiley was a fighter and he died fighting.' He thought of Wiley's gun saving his life. 'I think he'll rest in peace.'

He took her hand and they headed down the mountain together.

* * *

'Where will you go now, John Galley?' Yellow Bird asked as he helped Galley saddle up his horse.

Galley shrugged. 'We figure we might head north. Maybe set up a ranch. Sarah's a good rancher, you know.' He smiled at Sarah, waiting on her horse and talking to the Indian women she had gotten to know during her stay at the Sioux village.

Galley swung himself up onto his saddle and said, 'It's been good to know you, Yellow Bird.'

The medicine man nodded. 'My people are grateful to you, John Galley. The secret of our sacred mountain is safe. The Great Spirit was right; you are a man to be trusted.'

'Just what was that secret, anyhow?' Galley asked, feigning ignorance.

Yellow Bird shook his head. 'The flame-haired one was the only white man who knew of our secret and it has gone with him to the next life. Now only Sioux know the secret.' He picked up an armful of woven blankets and placed them on Galley's saddle. 'These are from my people to you and your woman.'

'Thanks,' Galley said. 'Oh, I almost forgot.' He pulled a small tin from his waistcoat and handed it to the medicine man. 'This is for you.' He spurred his horse forward and Sarah joined him, waving goodbye to the Sioux in the village behind them. They rode out along the mountains.

'Where are we headed, John?' Sarah asked.

He shrugged. 'I've been thinking it's time I settled down. So how are you fixed for running a ranch? Maybe up north?'

She considered for a moment and smiled. 'Sounds good to me. But where are we going to get the money to set up?'

Galley thought about the gold in his saddlebag. He wouldn't tell anyone where he had found it. 'I don't think that will be a problem,' he said.

★   ★   ★

Yellow Bird looked at the tin Galley had given him, wondering what it contained. Whatever it was, it would be something to remember the white man by. The white man who had communed with his spirits. He opened the lid and gasped in surprise as he saw the contents.

Inside, glinting in the tin, were tiny flakes of gold. And beside them was a folded up piece of paper. The medicine man unfolded it and read it.

Your secret is safe with me.

Yellow Bird laughed and closed the tin. The Great Spirit had been right. John Galley was a man to be trusted.

★ ★ ★

As they rode north, Galley looked at Sarah riding beside him and at the beautiful landscape around him.

Maybe now I live.

Yes.

Author's Afterword

In August 1895, a military expedition led by General George Custer discovered gold in the Black Hills. This precipitated a gold rush to the area and was the main cause of the second Sioux war.

The Ghost Dance religion went through a cycle of flourishing and waning, finally re-emerging in 1890, when the American government decided to repress the Indians' beliefs. This decision culminated in the massacre at Wounded Knee creek on 29th December 1890. Big Foot and Yellow Bird were killed on that cold day.

The Ghost Dance died with them.

We do hope that you have enjoyed reading this large print book.

Did you know that all of our titles are available for purchase?

We publish a wide range of high quality large print books including:
Romances, Mysteries, Classics
General Fiction
Non Fiction and Westerns

Special interest titles available in large print are:
The Little Oxford Dictionary
Music Book, Song Book
Hymn Book, Service Book

Also available from us courtesy of Oxford University Press:
Young Readers' Dictionary
(large print edition)
Young Readers' Thesaurus
(large print edition)

For further information or a free brochure, please contact us at:
Ulverscroft Large Print Books Ltd.,
The Green, Bradgate Road, Anstey,
Leicester, LE7 7FU, England.
Tel: (00 44) **0116 236 4325**
Fax: (00 44) **0116 234 0205**

Other titles in the
Linford Western Library:

THE CHISELLER

Tex Larrigan

Soon the paddle-steamer would be on its long journey down the Missouri River to St Louis. Now, all Saul Rhymer had to do was to play the last master-stroke of the evening. He looked at the mounting pile of gold and dollar bills and again at the cards in his hand. Then, looking around the table, he produced the deed to the goldmine in Montana. 'Let's play poker!' But little did he know how that journey back to St Louis would change his life so drastically.

THE ARIZONA KID

Andrew McBride

When former hired gun Calvin Taylor took the job of sheriff of Oxford County, New Mexico, it was for one reason only — to catch, or kill, the notorious Arizona Kid, and pick up the fifteen hundred dollars reward the governor had secretly offered. Taylor found himself on the trail of the infamous gang known as the Regulators, hunting down a man who'd once been his friend. The pursuit became, in every sense, a journey of death.

BULLETS IN
BUZZARDS CREEK

Bret Rey

The discovery of a dead saloon girl is only the beginning of Sheriff Jeff Gilpin's problems. Fortunately, his old friend 'Doc' Holliday arrives in Buzzards Creek just as Gilpin is faced by an outlaw gang. In a dramatic shoot-out the sheriff kills their leader and Holliday's reputation scares the hell out of the others. But it isn't long before the outlaws return, when they know Holliday is not around, and Gilpin is alone against six men . . .

THE YANKEE HANGMAN

Cole Rickard

Dan Tate was given a virtually impossible task: to save the murderer Jack Williams from the condemned cell. Williams, scum that he was, held a secret that was dear to the Confederate cause. But if saving Williams would test all Dan's ingenuity, then his further mission called for immense courage and daring. His life was truly on the line and if he didn't succeed, Horace Honeywell, the Yankee Hangman would have the last word!

MISSOURI PALACE

S. J. Rodgers

When ex-lawman Jim Williams accepts the post of security officer on the *Missouri Palace* river-boat, he finds himself embroiled in a power struggle between Captain J. D. Harris and Jake Farrell, the murderous boss of Willow Flats, who will stop at nothing to add the giant sidepaddler to his fleet. Williams knows that with no one to back him up in a straight fight with Farrell's hired killers, he must hit them first and hit them hard to get out alive.

THE CONRAD POSSE

Frank Scarman

The Conrad Posse, the famous group that had set about cleaning up a territory infested by human predators, was disbanding. The names of the infamous pistolmen hunted down by the Posse were now mostly a roll-call of the dead, but the name of the much sought Frank Jago was not among them. That proved to be a fatal mistake for it was not long before Jago took to his old trail of robbery and murder. Violence bred violence, and soon death stalked the land.